The

The Trial of Henry the 8th
By
Andrew Blair

Copyright 2022

Chapter One
England 1547

Henry knew he was dying. He knew it from looking at the frightened faces round him. They lied to him of course and told him that God would not allow Henry, King of England, to die so young. But the fear in their eyes told a different story.

They all feared for their positions and even their lives. Henry knew of the in-fighting, intrigue and jealousy in his court where one wrong step could result in execution. He knew because he had encouraged it. And it would be worse after his death.

But most all he knew he was dying because he felt a level of fear he had never felt before.

But why should he be fearful? He was an anointed King chosen by God himself. And had he not honoured God all his life? When he had broken from Rome it was because God had directed him to do so. He had risked his realm and his life but he had done God's will.

Only twice had he transgressed. His first marriage had been a sin but God had punished him by denying him a son. In his confusion he had been tempted by the devil in the form of Anne Boleyn. But he had conquered his demons and sent the witch to hell. And had God not forgiven him by then granting him a male heir?

But as he lay there, his breath weak and painful, he did feel real fear. What if he had been wrong? What if God was angry with him? It was not a new fear or even a new thought.

He had told no one of it of course-a King can never express doubts or show fear. But in weak moments such thoughts had entered his head like an invasive maggot into an apple. In his mind he dismissed them as the work of the devil and mostly he was free of them. But they always at some point came back and lately, as if sensing his weakness, with increasing frequency.

Did all men go through this as they lay dying? He had never thought of this before but now he realised they must do. Surely all those who had sinned had feared for their soul as they prepared for death. Was it enough to repent on your death-bed to escape an eternity in hell?

But he was not like all men. He was a King chosen by God. And through him God had done his work. He had broken from Rome because God had wanted him to. It was the false Pope who should fear death not he. If God had not wanted him to succeed, he would have struck him down then. The thought caused the fear to recede but it was still there as was a nagging doubt.

He looked round at the fearful faces that gazed down at him. He knew the terrible dilemma they faced. Henry had given instructions he wanted the last rites, but no one would bring the matter up. To discuss the Kings death was to wish the Kings death and this was treason. Had this not been one of the charges against Anne Boleyn and her lovers?

He tried to speak now, desperate for Cranmer to administer to him. But his voice was too weak to make himself understood. And now the fear turned to panic as he realised how close to death he was. His eyes fixed on his archbishop as he tried once again.

"Cranmer, you must..,"

He could hardly hear his own voice but all eyes turned to Cranmer and he stepped forward with a smile that he probably intended to be reassuring. He took Henry's hand.

"I am here my Liege."

Henry tried to clasp his hand but now he had little strength left. The room behind Cranmer seemed to fade away and Henry felt himself slipping away from his archbishop who was speaking.

"Put your trust in Christ my King and call upon his mercy. Though you cannot speak give me some token with your eyes or hand that you trust in the lord."

Henry stared at him and tried to speak but no words formed on his lips. Desperate now he summoned all his remaining strength to apply the smallest pressure to the archbishop's hand.

To his relief Cranmer's sad smile told him he had succeeded and then he, Henry, King of England, closed his eyes and his turbulent mortal life came to an end.

Chapter Two

Henry opened his eyes and then, dazzled by a strange light, instantly closed them again. He took a few breaths and was shocked by how strong they were. Indeed his whole body felt strong. Not as powerful as in his youth but stronger than he had felt in the years since his life-changing jousting accident.

The almost constant pain from his joints had gone as was the putrid smell of the pus-filled leg injury. Physically he felt incredible but as soon as he thought it the memory of Cranmer looking down at him with sad eyes came to him.

The feeling of disappointment was overwhelming. His regained health was just a dream and in a few minutes he would wake up in the bedroom in Whitehall and the pain and suffering would return. But at least he had confounded them all again. At least he was still alive. He had shown them once again that Tudor Kings do not die easily.

He opened his eyes again determined to enjoy the dream for however long it lasted. He stared at the strangely smooth ceiling. Gradually his eyes got used to the light. It was weird and somehow wonderful. It was like light on a midsummer day, but he was inside a building with no windows.

He glanced nervously round the room. The light seemed to come from small tubular glasses in the ceiling. The walls to the room were also smooth and painted in a light blue colour. They, like the rest of the room, were bare of ornaments, pictures or artefacts. Beside the bed he lay on there were just two uncomfortable looking chairs that were made of strange looking material and one small desk.

The bed was the most comfortable one he had ever slept on but it was also the smallest. Henry, King of England, did not sleep on beds designed for one.

It and the bareness of the room made him feel slightly uncomfortable. The room was functional and without character. It was like one of his ministers work rooms.

Despite the euphoria of his regained health, and of still being alive, he began to feel a strange sense of foreboding. He pushed back his blankets and stepped out of his bed. He was shocked to find himself dressed in jacket and trousers made of a thin cotton. They were comfortable, clean and smelt wonderful but it was not something a King would wear.

He was barefoot and the smooth floor felt cold. Beside the bed he saw two light looking shoes with a sort of felt bottom and cotton upper. He slipped them on and walked to the door. After a step he stopped; suddenly realising it was the first time he had walked unaided in months.

He felt a surge of joy at this but then he paused and somewhere in his consciousness he felt an overwhelming sense of fear. It took his breath away but then it was gone. No, that was wrong. It had retreated to the edge of his consciousness but it was still there, like a wisp of smoke he couldn't grasp.

He walked to the door. The handle was made of a smooth metal he had never seen before. The door was locked. He stared at it and then tried again to no avail. He admitted to himself that he had known it was going to be locked before he had even reached the door.

He walked back and sat on the bed. Now he was scared. It was not even the strangeness of the room or the dream itself. It was the fact he had been awake, in his dream at least, for some time now and no one had attended him. Henry was never left to fend for himself in the morning. Within moments of him waking he would have servants attending to his every need. But here he was alone.

He wanted to wake up now. He was no longer enjoying the dream and now the fear had returned to the forefront of his consciousness. He needed to wake up. He would rather the bloated body and the pus-filled leg than this. He would rather death than this.

He Henry, King of England, was locked in. He was a prisoner.

Chapter Three

He heard footsteps. He sat bolt upright on the bed and stared at the door. The footsteps stopped outside and there was a knock before it was immediately opened.

A man walked briskly in carrying a file. He placed it on the table and then smiled at Henry.

"Ahh Henry, glad to see you are up and about. Good show as we have an awful lot to do and very little time."

Henry stared at him in disbelief.

"Who... What are you?"

The man smiled again.

"I am a lawyer Henry, your lawyer in fact."

"But... But your attire, what are you wearing?"

"Ahh yes, I can see how that would be a bit of a shock. It is called a suit or, to be more exact, a bespoke suit. It is rather nice don't you think? Better than all that clobber you guys wore. What was all that ruff and pantaloons malarkey about?"

Henry looked at him in total confusion.

"Your speech... Where are you from?"

"I am from England old boy, only about 7 miles from Hampton Court as it happens."

"But... But no one speaks like you in England."

"Well language changes over time."

Henry felt his body tremble.

"What do you mean? "

"I mean Henry old boy, we are going to have to get used to each other's language. It is all English at the end of the day. All we have done is pared it down and cut out all the needless crap. God, how you guys went on."

"My guys?"

"Yes, you know. I have seen letters you have written and your ministers and mad off-spring. All this forthwith and henceforth bollocks. You people never used one word when you could use twenty."

"What do you mean by my off-spring?"

"You know, little protestant Edward, vengeful catholic Mary and sexually frustrated Elizabeth."

Henry was outraged.

"How dare you speak of my children that way? It is treason and you have not once called me Sire."

He marched to the door, beside himself with fury, and, when he was unable to open it, he banged his fists on the strange surface.

"GUARDS, GUARDS I WANT THIS MAN ARRESTED AND TAKEN TO THE TOWER."

He continued for several minute before turning back to see the man grinning at him while leaning on the chair.

"I am afraid all that King stuff doesn't work here Henry."

Henry glared at him. He was livid but the anger was laced with a deep fear.

"What do you mean?"

The man looked at him for several seconds and the grin left his face.

"Calm down and sit-down Henry. I will then explain a few things to you."

Henry stared back at him.

"I sit and you kneel."

"No Henry, no one is going to kneel to you here. Now sit down."

"You dare to give orders to a King?"

The man gave him a mocking smile.

"Yes, I dare. Now sit down."

"I will have you killed you cur,"

"No, you will not. Now sit down."

Henry was as stubborn as could be and the thought of obeying an order from a commoner offended his dignity. But he had no choice. He sat down on the bed.

The man moved the smaller chair in front of him and sat down.

"Henry, you are not King here."

"Who is the King? What traitor dares usurp me? Is it Norfolk?"

The man smiled.

"No, it is not Norfolk, but it might interest you to know that he dodged the date with the axeman you had planned for him. You really should have got rid of him earlier."

"Who would dare countermand my orders?."

"Henry, no one is King here and certainly not you."

Henry suddenly laughed.

"It does not matter you dog. This is just a dream, and you are not real."

The man sighed and closed his eyes for a second. When he opened them he looked at Henry with a new intensity.

"Henry, I know what you are going through and I know the fear and confusion you are feeling. I felt it myself and everyone does. Now normally I would indulge you. I would bring you to the reality of your situation gradually to lessen the shock. But we do not have time for that. Henry, you have to face up to what, in your heart of hearts, you already know. Henry, this is not a dream and you are never going to wake up on that bed in Whitehall."

Henry stared at him as his body went cold. He felt an indescribable panic rising in his very being. The man was right. He did know. He had known from the point he had woken up in the strange room. But, even now, he could not bring himself to say it.

"You mean... You mean...."

He stared at the man in despair.

"Please…,"

The man nodded slowly.

"Henry, you are not going to wake up in the bed in Whitehall. You are not going to because that was your death-bed. You are dead Henry. You died on that bed."

Henry continued to stare at him and neither spoke for a long time. Strangely, now the words had been spoken and the reality faced, the panic subsided a little. The man waited in silence as Henry tried to process the devastating information. Henry had never felt so weak and scared. Eventually he found the courage to speak.

"So, what is this place?"

The man gave him a half-smile.

"That was quite impressive. You handled that fairly well. Most get very hysterical at some point."

"I am a King and a King of England at that."

The man smiled.

"Well, I think you need to use the past tense here, but I will admit you did show a courage I didn't expect from you."

"You think ill of me?"

"Yes of course, pretty much everyone thinks ill of you,"

Henry looked at him.

"Why would that be?"

"Do you really not know?"

"Is it because I broke with Rome?"

"No, not really. God, this is going to be challenging if you think that is the worst thing on your charge list."

Henry looked at him-the panic level again rising.

"My charge list? What do you mean by charge list? What is this place?"

The man gave him a grim smile.

"It is a holding cell Henry. It is a bit like being sent to the tower in your day but a whole lot more comfortable. You will stay here until your trial."

"A TRIAL. YOU DARE TRY ME. I AM HENRY, KING OF ENGLAND"

"I thought we had cleared all that up. You are not King here and you are facing a trial."

Henry stared at him in confusion.

"But...But what am I accused of?"

"It would probably be easier to say what aren't you accused of but multiple counts of murder are top of the list."

"MURDER. ARE YOU MAD? I HAVE MURDERED NO ONE"

The man smiled.

"Well, that is for a jury to decide."

"But... But who have I supposedly murdered?"

"There are too many to mention but Anne Boleyn for one and her alleged lovers. Thomas Cromwell as well. There are quite a few others. You are also charged with false imprisonment of your first wife."

"But I did not kill them. They were executed under the law. And as for Catherine I was her husband and King. If I wanted to confine her to a house as punishment for disobeying me that is my business. I broke no law."

"You really better hope the jury sees it your way."

Henry looked at him.

"But this is ridiculous. What does it matter if I am found guilty or not? I am already dead."

The man looked at him for several seconds.

"I am surprised that someone from your deeply religious age would ask such a question. I would expect it from someone from my time because we are quite dismissive of religious mumbo-jumbo. But you are a very religious man Henry. You must know what will happen if you are found guilty."

Henry stared at him in disbelief and then he felt real terror. It seemed to creep up his whole body. He felt paralysed with fear. It was some time before he could find the strength to move his lips.

"You mean... You mean...."

The man once again gave him a grim smile.

"Yes Henry. If you are found guilty your soul will reside in the place you call hell for all eternity."

Chapter Four

"You cannot try a King. Only God can judge a King."

"Strangely enough, about 100 years after you snuffed it one of your descendants said the same thing to an English court. A few days later, after being found guilty of treason, they chopped his head off."

Henry stared at him in confusion.

"This is mad. It cannot be real. You cannot be real."

"It is very real Henry."

"But...But what do you mean a hundred years after I died? I only died yesterday."

The man smiled in the irritating way Henry was becoming accustomed to.

"Well, it is all about perspective. Also time is very different here. In fact, it does not really exist at all. From your perspective you died yesterday. From my perspective you died about 450 years ago."

Henry looked at him for a long time.

"You are insane. You are a mad man."

The man laughed.

"I am afraid not Henry. School children have been learning about you for 400 years and, I have to be honest, most of them don't like what they have learned."

"Maybe it is I that is insane. None of this is real. It cannot be."

"Henry, as I said before, we don't have time for this. I understand how mind-blowing all this must be but just do me a favour and go along with it. It doesn't matter if you don't think it is real. If I wait until you realise the truth it will be too late."

"But... But I do not understand."

The man sighed.

"Henry, all you have to do is to concentrate your mind on these facts. Your actions in your life-time are going to be judged by a jury. I have drawn the shortest bloody straw ever and been appointed to defend you. If you are found guilty by the court your soul will be cast into hell for all eternity. Now understandably you are going to find all that hard to believe but that doesn't matter right now. If you think it a game, fine. But just humour me and play the game."

"What jury? Who are these people?"

"Yes, well here we have a problem, and it is a biggie. The jury will be selected from people closer to my time than yours. I argued against this of course but the judge went with the prosecution."

"That does not seem fair."

"It is not fair. I am not going to lie. It is a disaster for our case. Every member of the jury will have read the history of your life. There have been hundreds of books written about you and countless TV and movie depictions. Pretty much all of them cast you as a monster."

"TV and movie depictions?"

The man smiled.

"Yes, I will explain about them later."

Henry was bewildered.

"But why would I be cast as a monster?"

"It stems from your habit of chopping off the head of anyone who pisses you off."

"But they broke the law. They all had a fair trial."

"No Henry. They all had a trial. There was nothing fair about any of them. No one was going to go against your wishes as they would know their head would soon be on the block if they did. This is the reason the judge refused my petition to have a jury from your time. He thought that, even with them being dead, they would still be too scared to condemn you."

"That is a damnable lie. I respected the law."

"No Henry, you made the law."

Henry stared at him for a minute.

"What chance do I have when you, who are supposed to defend me, think me guilty?"

"Oh, don't worry I will try my damnedest to get you off. I am very good and I have a reputation to keep up. It is another reason why the judge decided you would be tried under the twenty-first century English law system. It is as fair as it can be, and a central pillar is that everyone is entitled to a fair trial and legal representation. I am duty bound to defend you to the best of my abilities. "

"Even if you think me guilty?"

"Yes,"

"But you do consider me guilty?"

He smiled in reply.

"That my dear Henry is an irrelevant question I am not going to answer."

Henry considered him for some time.

"What is your name?"

"Lightfoot, Duncan Lighfoot."

"The Twenty-First Century? This is insane. It cannot be real."

"Like I said, just go along with it until you realise it is true."

Henry knew it was true. He was totally confused by the alien-like man and the incredible idea that he, Henry, King of England, had to face a trial for his very soul. But even though he could not bring himself to admit it even to himself, the fear that chilled his very bones told him it was true. Also the man's complete lack of respect for him told its own tale. Even in his dreams no one spoke to him in such a way.

"Who is King in your time?"

"I am dead Henry. Everyone here is dead but when I died Queen Elizabeth the 2nd was on the throne. She still is in fact.

Do you want to hazard a guess as to who was Queen Elizabeth the 1st?"

Henry stared at him.

"My Elizabeth. You mean my Elizabeth became Queen?"

"Sure did and history considers her a highly successful one. She had a very clever first minister called William Cecil and , unlike you, she wasn't stupid enough to chop his head off."

Henry felt his anger flare.

"How dare you speak to me so?"

Lightfoot smiled.

"You are dead Henry and in my opinion I speak the truth. Of all the bad decisions you made, killing Thomas Cromwell was surely the worst."

Henry stared at him silently. He hated admitting to any mistake.

"You are correct. He had vexed me by committing me to marry the Cleves woman and then Norfolk and the others persuaded me against him. He managed things for me very well. It was never the same after he died. What happened to my son?"

Lightfoot looked at him grimly.

"I am afraid he died aged fifteen."

Henry was silent. All that upheaval for nothing. He remembered his joy at the birth. He had done it. He had sired an heir to continue the Tudor name. But, even in death, God had punished him.

"So then Mary became Queen. I suppose she took England back to Rome."

"She attempted to but Edward had tried to prevent that by changing your succession decree. He named Lady Jane Grey as his successor as she was protestant."

Henry glared at him.

"How dare he do such a thing?"

"He probably had power hungry men such as her father-in-law manipulating him, but most historians think your son was the driving force. You may have changed England's religion to suit your carnal desires Henry, old boy, but there were repercussions. Your son, guided by Cranmer, was a devout protestant and he wasn't about to hand England back to the Catholics."

"How dare you? It was not for carnal desire that I split from Rome. A King must be master in his own land."

Lightfoot smiled.

"Whatever, it didn't matter anyway as the people, and certain members of the council, rebelled and put Mary on the throne. Poor Jane Grey, who was just a pawn in her father-in-Laws game, ended up headless."

"Mary should not have killed her."

"To be fair she held off doing so for some time but the problem was there was a faction of the new religion plotting to other-throw Mary and the next legitimate heir was Jane. Mary was persuaded that to stop the plots she had to get rid of her. As it happened it didn't matter as the plotters just moved onto Elizabeth after Jane's execution."

"And they succeeded, and Mary was beheaded?"

"No, they did not succeed. Mary was determined to reconcile England with Rome and started slaughtering anyone opposed to it. That included Cranmer amongst many others although this had more to do with the way he helped you divorce her Mother. England must have been a hot place during her reign because so many heretics were burnt at the stake. She is known in the history books as Bloody Mary."

Henry sighed.

"She was always bitter. I should never have put her in the succession while she remained devoted to Rome. Did she succeed in taking England back into the catholic fold."

"Yes, she came to an agreement with the Pope and even married Philip the 2nd of Spain. But the burning of every prominent protestant made her, the Spanish and the catholic religion very unpopular. And of course, ultimately she died without an heir and was forced to go along with your order of succession and make Elizabeth, who was protestant, Queen. She, like you, then became head of the Church of England as well as the monarch."

"Well I am glad at that although I didn't want England to go to the new religion. That was not my intention."

"I know but that is what you set in motion when you broke from Rome so you could marry Anne Boleyn."

"And so her daughter became Queen. How did she fare?"

"Well, apart from our present Queen I don't like any of our monarchs because most became homicidal, self-entitled despots. But there is no doubt that she steadied the ship after the madness you set in motion. England also became a world power with the beginnings of an Empire. She also won out against her very considerable enemies."

"Did she honour me?"

"Yes, in public at least. Whatever she thought of you in private is open to conjecture but there is no record of her ever criticising you. But when she died it was discovered that in a ring that never left her finger there was an image of her mother."

"Her mother was a witch."

"Yes, you have mentioned that before. The thing is Henry you have to stop doing so."

"Why, I believe it to be true,"

"I don't believe you and, more importantly, the jury won't believe you. They will be willing to accept that belief in witches was wide-spread in your time. But the jury will believe you accepted the trumped up charges against her so you could rid yourself of her and marry Jane Seymour. The fact you married her on the very day Boleyn was executed sort of reinforces that belief don't you think?"

"They were not trumped up charges. She was guilty."

Lightfoot looked at him and then nodded.

"I will be trying to convince the jury of that fact Henry. Well, I will try to challenge their certainty that she was innocent anyway. And, believe it or not, I don't think it is impossible to do that."

Chapter Five

Henry stared at the strange glass screen in complete shock. When Lightfoot had carried it in and then brought it to life with the implement in his hand Henry had almost passed out. It had terrified him and, to his eternal shame, he had cowered in the corner. What dark sorcery was this?

But that was twelve hours ago and Henry was no longer scared of what Lightfoot called a TV screen. But he was stunned, outraged and fearful of the incredible moving pictures that were on the screen. Lightfoot had warned him.

"You are not going to like it Henry but this is how you have been portrayed for centuries. The TV is a new invention but there are books and plays going back to not long after your death. I am showing them to you to make you aware of what we are up against."

It was weird and unsettling to see himself portrayed by other people. Many were absurd and even ridiculous. Some, such as the one showing him as an ill-mannered lout throwing chicken legs about, were outrageous. But a few of them were uncomfortably close to the mark.

How could they know so much? Lightfoot told him that royal letters were preserved as were those from other prominent men. Some diaries had also survived and a lot of court documents had been carefully archived. But some private conversations he had had with, among others Cromwell, Wolsey and Thomas More were portrayed broadly accurately. How could that be?

But it was also so wrong. It was so very wrong. The moving pictures were not remotely fair to him. What Lightfoot had called documentaries by prominent historians were a little more balanced but even here he was shown as a selfish despot. In all the others he was basically a cruel monster.

The door opened and Lightfoot walked in with his infuriating smile.

"Pretty bad hey? How does it feel to be one of the most despised monarchs in English history?"

Henry stood up and exploded.

"THIS IS LIES, ALL LIES. THIS IS NOT ME. I WAS A JUST RULER."

Lightfoot just smiled at his rage.

"Really Henry. And what parts are they lying about pray tell?"

Henry was exasperated.

"All of it. All the people who died were traitors."

"Traitors to who?"

"To me of course and to the nation."

"Had they not all served you well up to the point they were accused of treason? Wolsey and More were your favourite churchmen until you decided to break from the Pope. It seems to me, and it will seem to the jury, that they only became traitors to you when they refused to become traitors to their faith and to themselves."

"But... But it was their duty to do so. I was their King."

"Was it Catherine's duty to give you a son? Was it Anne Boleyn's?"

Henry looked at him in confusion.

"Yes...Yes it was,"

Lightfoot sighed.

"Sit down Henry."

Henry glared at him but then did as he asked.

"Henry, what I am about to say to you is the most important thing I ever will. Make no mistake, your very soul depends on you heeding this advice. I can mount the most brilliant defence ever, but it will be meaningless unless you do so. Even if you do we are massive under-dogs in the coming trial. But if you don't I have zero chance of saving you soul or reputation."

Henry stared at him. The solemn words, coming from a man who rarely seemed serious, chilled him. He nodded.

"Go on,"

"Henry, you cannot go into that court room and behave as the jury has been conditioned to expect you to behave. You can't be the arrogant, no-one else matters but me Henry that they expect. If you do your soul will burn in hell for all eternity. That is the bottom line."

"How can I not be me. You talk like a fool."

"Henry, the jury who will decide your fate believe in something called democracy. In England now parliament has all the power. Any party winning an general election has to ask the Queens permission to form a government. In theory she can refuse and choose who she wants as Prime minister. But only in theory. If she did so it would be the end of the monarchy as the people won't stand for it. She can never go against her government."

"That is ridiculous. What is the point of being Queen if she has no power?"

"She serves the people Henry. She is an ambassador respected round the world. She gives her government wise council but she is just a figurehead. She sets an example to her people. It is called a constitutional monarchy."

"But what has that to do with me?"

"Henry, we have a constitutional monarchy because we rejected your kind of absolute monarchy. In the modern England every citizen has one vote. The Queen has one vote as does the guy who cleans the privy's. And these are the kind of people who will be on the jury. If you go in there claiming everything you did was ok because you were King they will hate you. And nothing I say after that will have any effect. You will be doomed."

"So my fate will be decided by uneducated peasants? What madness is this? Privy cleaners having the same power as a King! This place is insane. What of the great families? What of the nobility?"

"Wrong attitude Henry, really wrong attitude."

"I don't understand all this. How can lowly peasants judge a King?"

"They are not judging a King Henry. They are judging a man."

"But then what chance do I have?"

"As I said, you have a small chance but that depends on you appearing before them as a man, not a King."

"Why would that make a difference?"

Lightfoot smiled at him.

"It makes a difference because men, all men, make mistakes. What you have to do Henry old boy is something you appear never to have done. You have to acknowledge that you are a fallible human being who, just like them, makes mistakes."

"You want me to grovel?"

"No Henry, I don't want you to grovel. I want you to be fair-minded. I want you to be calm and considered. I want you to remain calm when the prosecution accuses you of crimes. In short Henry, I want you to knock the jury off balance by being the total opposite of what they expected."

Henry looked at him. He could see the sense in Lightfoot's words, but he still thought them repellent.

"No. I cannot be someone I am not. I am quick to anger, I always have been. And I will not grovel. I will meet my accusers, and those who would judge me, as Henry King of England. And I will meet my fate, if judged guilty, the same way."

Chapter Six

"But that is not strictly true is it, Henry?"

"What is not true?"

"You were not always quick to anger. You were once very popular Henry. All the history books say the same. In your youth, before your older brother's death, your peers, the court and the common people all loved and respected you. You were seen as fair, noble and loyal to your friends."

Henry was quiet.

"That was long ago. The weight of the crown of England is a heavy burden."

"Well, the weight has gone now and that man is still there inside you. You need him back. That is the Henry you need to be in the court room."

"But how can I turn back time?"

"You don't have to. All you have to do is remember. How do you feel now?"

"I feel great. My leg that has been agony for years no longer hurts. I am not as corpulent."

"Corpulent! You are no longer as obscenely fat. That is what I negotiated with the judge. The prosecution wanted you as you died and I wanted you to be in the full bloom of your youth. This was the compromise. Your physical and mental condition now is as it was a month before your jousting accident in 1536."

"Well, I thank you for that. But why did the judge refuse your petition?"

"The prosecution argued that the youthful Henry did not commit the crimes he is being accused of. It was decided that it would confuse the jury if you appeared so at odds with your reputation. What they really meant was that you would appear as a sympathetic and likeable character. That is why I urge you to remember the way you were."

"So how did you win the compromise?"

"The judge agreed with me that if you turned up at court as you had died it might constitute an unfair trial. The jury would be prejudiced against you from the start as you would appear to them to be the tyrant they have been conditioned to expect."

"But why that date?"

"I wanted it earlier-long before your divorce from Catherine and your break from Rome. But the date is important because the jousting accident is seen as a big turning point in your life."

"Why so?"

"I will explain more later. But what I want you to do now is ask yourself this. How would the younger Henry have handled the major events that came later in your life."

Henry thought about that.

"What difference would that make?"

"Leave that to me. The important thing is for you to really consider it. And Henry, you must be honest with yourself. Look at your life from the view point of your youth and acknowledge your mistakes. You will not have to grovel in court but you are going to have to admit that people suffered at your hands and you were not always fair to them."

"I was always fair,"

"No Henry, you weren't. And deep inside you know it. That is bombastic, self-entitled Henry speaking. Every man makes mistakes. Every man is capable of cruelty. And every man has regrets. You are no different and nor are the jury. But before you can convince others of your regrets you must admit them to yourself. Just give it a chance. I will leave you for several hours and I want you to examine your life and your decisions. Remember the young, noble good man you once were and become him again."

Henry nodded slowly.

"Ok, I will try,"

Lightfoot smiled.

"You have done it before haven't you Henry? Most people near death look back at their lives with some degree of regret."

"But we can change nothing. If a jury finds me guilty of crimes they cannot be any lesser of a crime because I regret them. And that is not an admission. I still say I committed no crimes."

"It might matter Henry. But you must truly regret some of the things you did and how you behaved in the later part of your life. This is not like an earthly court in that the jury will know if you are being dishonest. Don't ask me how they know but they will. They don't even know how they do that themselves. It is just that in this place, where your very soul is a stake, there is no hiding place."

"But then I am doomed. What was considered fair justice in my time is considered murder here. How can I prevail against that? I will tell the truth and I will be condemned."

"The judge will allow me to use that defence to a certain degree. But he will put limits on me. But, if the jury is convinced of your regret, I can make a case on nearly every accusation. But Henry, this is about more than the individual accusations. It basically boils down to whether you were an evil man in your life-time. That is pretty much the bottom line."

Henry stared at him in astonishment. It was what he had been told from childhood."

"So the Priests were right. Everyman is judged."

"I don't think the churchmen of any faith imagine it is like this but you are broadly correct. Most do not get a trial like this though."

"Is that because I am a King?"

Lightfoot smiled.

"Put your ego back in the box Henry. No, it is because you face the ultimate punishment. It is not considered right to condemn anyone to such a terrible fate without allowing them to defend themselves."

"Are my perceived crimes so bad? I never personally killed anyone? And I maintain that they were all guilty of crimes against me."

"I would agree that there have been thousands worse than you. There was one a few years ago who presided over the biggest genocide in human history. He caused a world war that resulted in the deaths of about 50 million. He bult death camps in which six million men women and children, most of them Jewish, were gassed to death. I pity the poor bastard who had to defend him."

Henry stared at him in shock.

"You are insane. There are not that many people on the whole of the Earth."

"There are now Henry."

"So am I considered like him?"

"No, but you are considered a tyrant like he was. And you are not just being blamed for the deaths in your life-time. There was the carnage that were the direct result of your decisions. Hundreds of Catholics died when your son was King and even more Protestants died when Mary was on the throne. It is your sheer selfishness that is on trial. You cared not one bit about the effects your decisions had on your friends or subjects. It is said that the definition of evil is a lack of empathy for other people. This is what you are accused of."

"That is not true."

"Isn't it? Did you ever consider the terror of the people facing the axeman? Did you ever imagine the sheer agony of someone being burnt at the stake? Did the feelings of their children never move you to tears?"

Henry stared at him for a long time. No, he never had. Cromwell had had children. Eventually he shook his head.

"A great King must often make hard decisions. He cannot let emotions get in the way. What kind of ruler would I be if I spared a man convicted of treason because he had a child?"

Now Lightfoot looked at him for a long while. His gaze was penetrating and uncomfortable.

"Henry, did you never consider the terror of those people who you condemned to die? Some of them had been loyal friends for years."

Henry tried to hold his gaze but couldn't do so. What was happening to him? He knew who Lightfoot was referring to. Henry Norris, Francis Weston and William Brereton. All had been his friends. He nodded slowly.

"No, I never did."

Lightfoot sighed and stood up.

"Well Henry, I think you should heed my earlier advice and do just that."

Chapter Seven

It was true. They had all been his friends. But only now, after his own death, did he question their guilt. There was strong evidence against them and he had not been blind to the spell Boleyn had cast over them. If she could seduce a King she could seduce anyone. Some of Anne's ladies in waiting had spoken of furtive, illicit meetings between her and the named men. And Smeaton, the musician who had confessed to sexual relations with the Queen, had named them. They were probably guilty.

But maybe they weren't.

Most of the ladies of Anne's court hated her and those that didn't were aware that she was out of favour with the King. Also, Smeaton had only confessed after spending the night in the company of Thomas Cromwell. Was he tortured? Henry had never asked that question because he knew what the answer might be. He had intimated to Cromwell months earlier that he wanted out of the marriage.

On balance he still thought them guilty. And the adultery was not the worst part of it. Norris and the witch were heard talking about Henry's death and how Norris might replace him in Anne's bed.

When the gossip from the ladies had reached him he had asked Cromwell to investigate. Had he in some way made it clear to his chief fixer that he wanted a positive outcome that would see him free of Anne Boleyn? In his heart he knew the answer but he was still unwilling to face it. And had Cromwell taken the opportunity to rid himself of some of his own enemies at Court?

No, he doubted that. It was still much more likely that they were guilty. It was his instinct as much as anything. He had seen the looks that passed between Boleyn and the accused courtiers. She had known what she was doing. She knew it would enrage him and make him feel a cuckold even if he wasn't one at that point. She had been playing a game. She had used them to make him jealous. But it was a very dangerous game and they had been stupid to be drawn into it. Stupid or, more likely, bewitched.

But what of George Boleyn, her brother? The siblings were unusually close but would he really have committed incest with his own sister? Yes, because, as had been made clear to him, she could pass off a male offspring of such a union as the King's own. That would be a heinous crime but he would not have put it past her as she would be aware of his anger at her not giving birth to a male heir.

But Henry also knew that having George holding high office after his sister was executed for treason would be awkward to say the least. Cromwell would know this as well and he was never fond of loose strings.

Henry remembered Lightfoot's advice. What would the young Henry have done? The answer was obvious. He would have given them a chance to prove their innocence. He would have been distraught at the news of his friends betrayal rather than euphoric that there was now a way out of his marriage. This thought made him pause. How had he got to be so uncaring?

The young Henry had been kind and loyal to his friends. A young Henry would have been outraged by the accusations rather than glad of them. He stood up. A panel had opened in the wall and through a window he could see a meadow. There were deer and it reminded him of the view from Hampton Court. It was beautiful but Lightfoot had told him it was not real.

He felt better than he had done in a very long time. The last few years of his life had been agony but now he felt healthy and strong. It wasn't quite like his youth when he had been the tallest and strongest man at his Father's court. But it was at least a reminder of the man he had once been.

But it wasn't just his health that had been different then. People spoke well of him and meant it. Looking back his friends could not forget he was a Prince but they had no need to fear him. He had been quick to anger but, unlike his later years, it soon passed and he would not hold any bitterness to those who had caused his outburst.

Even after Arthur died and he became heir to the throne little changed where his friends, teachers and even servants were concerned. He loved being liked and respected by all. How had he become this vengeful, bitter and deeply unhappy man?

Being King was hard. At the outset of his reign he didn't want anything to change. He had had noble ambitions. His Father had ended the long struggle with the house of York and now he would consolidate that victory. He would build bridges with his Father's former enemies but he would also sire a child to ensure the continuation of the Tudor line. The failure to do so with Catherine was obviously where the journey from a young, optimistic popular Prince to a bitter, petulant and hated King had begun.

But could he not be excused that? Could not some allowance me made? For years he had failed in the most important duty of a King-to provide an heir. How could he not turn bitter at fate's cruel joke?

A bell went off and he looked round in confusion. It sounded again and then a smiling Lightfoot entered.

"It is called a door-bell Henry. You are meant to either open the door, ask who it is or just let me in."

"What kind of jail is it when the jailer has to ask permission to enter?"

"A very different one to those in your time. I have even brought you a menu so you can choose what you want to eat."

Henry suddenly realised he was hungry.

"But I am dead. How can I be hungry?"

Lightfoot laughed.

"This is a strange place. But the authorities obviously like it to be a pleasant experience. That will undoubtedly change if you are found guilty. But the judge has decided you shall think and feel exactly like you would at the date he decided on. So your physical and mental condition is the same as it was in 1536 before your accident."

"How do I understand your speech and you mine? You say words I have never heard of and I understand them."

"The judge decided you could not have a fair trial if you could not understand modern speech."

"Is he God?"

Lightfoot smiled.

"No, he is not God and it will not be he who decides your fate. It will be the jury. His job is just to ensure it is fair."

"But I cannot see how it can be fair if the jury have already made up their mind."

"We are certainly up against it but that is not going to change. How did you get on with the exercise I set you?"

Henry hesitated, reluctant to share his thoughts.

"You have to be honest with me Henry. I need to know what is in your head and I need to know if you look back with any regrets."

"Although I still think them probably guilty I regret I did not give Norris, Weston, and Brereton more chance to prove their innocence."

"Well that's a start at least. What about George Boleyn?"

"I think he was in league with his sister. But I suppose you are right and I should have had Cromwell investigate more."

"There is one thing you have to keep in mind Henry. Thomas Cromwell is not on trial here, you are. He has, or will, almost certainly face a trial of his own but it is not this one. You can blame him to a certain extent, but you were King and he was an advisor only. You didn't have to take that advice or accept his evidence."

"But he was my chief minister. When he presented his evidence I could not go against it."

"The prosecution is going to say the evidence was weak and I have to agree with them. They are going to say you were over-eager to accept the evidence because a guilty verdict meant you could be rid of Anne Boleyn and free to marry Jane Seymour. The bottom line is the buck stops with you not Thomas Cromwell."

"Just because the outcome benefited me doesn't mean she and they were not guilty."

"That is true. But can I ask you a question?"

"Yes, of course,"

"Do you now have some understanding, and even sympathy, for your friends as they faced their fate?"

Henry hesitated. What would it have been like? They had been powerful men basking in a King's friendship one minute and then, just days later, they were walking towards the axeman? The terror must have been terrible and how would it have been for their families. And not just them. So many had faced the same ordeal. Why had their plight, even though they were guilty of treason, not affected him before?"

"Yes, I do," he said quietly.

"Well that is interesting and I want you to hold that thought. I have a list of the charges against you. I want you to read through them in the same mind-set as you have now. It is very important that you do so and, in the first case at least, you might find it very difficult."

"What is the first charge?

"I will come to that in a minute. What will happen in court is that the prosecution will set out the charge against you and then, before they move on to the next charge, I will defend you against it. At the end both me and the prosecution lawyer will present final arguments and then the jury will decide your fate. We have two weeks to prepare for the trial."

Henry stared at him. With his new found health and the pleasant surroundings, along with the lifting of the massive weight of Kingship, he had begun to feel comfortable. He had forgotten why he was here and the ordeal he faced. But he was a King and he would face his accusers like a King should.

"Ok Lightfoot. Two weeks it is. What is the first charge?"

Lightfoot smiled.

"That's better Henry. I am liking that attitude. But I urge you to search your very soul and be honest with yourself. And remember, think like a man and not a King as you will be judged by ordinary men and women."

Henry was amazed.

"Women on a Jury!"

"Yes Henry, and that is going to be especially important where the first charge is concerned."

"But how can women judge the affairs of men?"

"Men and women have equal rights here and in most countries on Earth. And Henry, they really don't like seeing their fellow women badly treated."

Henry stared at him.

"What is the first charge?"

"The first charge Henry is that you divorced your first wife, Catherine of Aragon, on a false premise. You also asked her to lie under oath to support that premise. You are further charged that after the divorce you imprisoned her for the rest of her life and only very rarely let her see her daughter. The final charge is that when she died your celebrations were cruel, petulant, vulgar and not befitting a decent man let alone a King."

Chapter Eight

The case against Henry the 8th in regard to Catherine of Aragon.
The Prosecution.

"When did you first meet Catherine of Aragon Mr. Tudor?"

Henry stared at the foreign looking woman in astonishment. He looked at Lightfoot who smiled and shrugged his shoulders as if to say I told you so. He had warned him the day before the trial.

"She is English born but her parents were from what is now called India. You knew it as Hindustan. Her parents came to England to escape poverty. They worked incredibly hard to ensure their daughter got an education. And she did not let them down. From a poor state school she ended up with a top degree from Oxford university. Do not in any way under-estimate her. I very much doubt you have ever met anyone as intelligent."

"Oxford, Wolsey's Oxford? I know of it. It was never intended to have women studying there."

"Well, times change old boy. After many centuries of struggle women now have the same basic rights as men and no one epitomises that struggle more than council for the prosecution Amira Hussein."

"You mean she will hate me?"

"No, she will not hate you. That would be an emotional response that might interfere with her job. But she will try her very best to prove you guilty and her best is very, very good."

"But... But she is just a woman and from a heathen country."

"If you let that prejudice show we are finished before we start. And she will try to get you to make it show. She will rile and insult you. Do not in any way rise to her bait."

"Is she better than you?"

Lightfoot smiled.

"Well, I would say no but I am a cocky bastard and pretty much no one would agree with me?"

"Then what chance do we have?"

"We have a small chance Henry because, unlike your trials, you are innocent until proven guilty. The onus is on her to prove your guilt beyond reasonable doubt."

"But you state the jury have already made up their minds about me."

"I am not going to lie, that is a huge problem. But, and it is a big but, we can hopefully open their minds a little if you present a different Henry to the one expected."

Henry remembered this advice but the opening question from the woman deeply offended him. He tried to keep his voice calm.

"I am King of England. You will please address me as such."

The woman smiled.

"No, there are no Kings in this courtroom. You can either be addressed as Mr or by your first name."

Henry fought to keep his temper in check. How could this brown-skinned little woman insult him so? He glared at her but she just smiled at him expectantly. She was good-looking-beautiful even but, at that point she seemed like a serpent poised to strike. He looked at Lightfoot who glared back at him. He nodded at the woman.

"I prefer Henry,"

He saw her eyes widen slightly in surprise. He looked back at Lightfoot who gave him a nod of approval.

"So Henry, could you answer the question please. When did you first meet Catherine of Aragon?"

"I first met her in 1501 when she arrived in England to marry my older brother Arthur."

"And how old were you both at that point."

 "I was ten and Catherine was fifteen."

"And what were your first impressions"

"I liked her very much and thought her beautiful."

"Your brother was fourteen at the time I believe."

"That is correct."

"And he died at fifteen just five months after his wedding?"

"That is also correct."

"I understand that your Father, Henry the 7th, arranged the marriage between you and your brother's widow and that he had to get special dispensation from the Pope to allow this. Is that correct?"

Henry inwardly groaned. He knew where this was going.

"That is correct."

"And how did he get this special dispensation?"

"I believe you know the answer to that. From what I have seen and read everyone knows the answer."

The woman smiled.

"Please humour me, Henry."

"He got it because Catherine swore that the marriage between her and Arthur was never consummated."

"And the Pope accepted this?"

"Yes,"

"Did Catherine lie Henry?"

Henry was stunned by the starkness of the question even though Lightfoot had warned him that it would be asked. The woman, sensing his discomfort, smiled.

"It was not a case of lying,"

The woman laughed and turned to the jury.

"It was not a case of lying! Really Henry? I know she was just fifteen but I think she would be aware if she had had intercourse or not."

The Jury laughed along with the prosecutor. Henry felt his face redden and his anger grow. He looked at Lightfoot who made a gesture with his hands that meant calm down. He remembered what his lawyer had told him to say.

"What I meant was that she was put under huge pressure by my Father to say what he wanted. My Father could be very intimidating."

"So, you are saying that Catherine was so scared of defying your Father, Henry the 7th, that she was willing to lie under oath?"

"Yes,"

"No, sorry Henry but that does not wash. Your first wife, Catherine of Aragon, was one of the most pious women in history. She may have been frightened by your Father but she would have been much more scared of her God. She was also not a woman easily intimidated as you found out many years later when you asked her to swear that her first marriage was indeed consummated. She defied you and refused to lie."

Henry knew it was true. Despite what he said to others he had always known. Catherine would never have lied under oath. He hated to admit it but Lightfoot had advised him it would be a terrible mistake to brand Catherine a liar.

"I accept now that she told the truth. At the time I was convinced my marriage was unlawful in God's eyes. It is stated in the bible that if a man marries his brother's wife, the couple would be childless. I took that to mean Catherine's first marriage was indeed consummated."

The woman paused. Henry, as Lightfoot had advised him, did not look at the jury. Then the woman smiled again as if to show she understood that this would not be as easy as predicted and she would accept the challenge.

"But your marriage was not childless. You had a daughter, Mary."

"But it did not produce a son."

The woman smiled.

"Oh, I see, Women don't count."

She smiled at the jury, some of whom laughed. Then she continued.

"So the Pope upheld the decision made by his predecessor and decreed that the first marriage had not been consummated. In his, and God's eyes, your marriage to Catherine was lawful and he could not grant you an annulment."

"That is true but there were other forces at play. At the time, the Pope was the prisoner of Charles the 5th, the Holy Roman Emperor, who was Catherine's nephew. "

"So you believe the Pope's refusal to grant an annulment was as much political as spiritual?"

"Yes, I believe so."

"I am not sure that it is relevant as it is your behaviour that is being judged not the Popes. So, after that you decided to split from Rome, dump centuries of papal rule and make yourself head of the church of England. All to allow you to divorce Catherine. In today's terms we call that the nuclear option. Did it never cross your mind that it all may have been a tad selfish?"

Henry paused. Lightfoot had instructed him to count to ten whenever he felt his anger rise. He had also coached him on how to answer this question and many others.

"Not at the time, no I didn't. I can see now how people could have construed it that way. It clearly benefited me personally but, as I say, there were political implications too. The Pope was a prisoner of a man who could be seen as an international rival of mine. He also had a personal interest in the matter as he was closely related to Catherine."

"So, you are saying you split from the Roman Catholic church not because you wanted to dump Catherine to marry Anne Boleyn but because of politics?"

As she said this she again smiled at the jury, most of whom returned her smile. Henry once again counted to ten.

"I did not split from the Roman Catholic Church. I died a Roman Catholic. And, while my desire to have my first marriage annulled was the reason I appealed to the Pope, his refusal highlighted a problem in that I was not sovereign in my own land. It might have been acceptable to have the Pope as the adjudicator in religious matters but he could hardly go against the wishes of his captor. This meant that the man who ultimately held the power in England was Charles the 5th, the Holy Roman Emperor. This was not acceptable to me or in the interests of my country."

There was an audible murmur from the jury. This time Henry glanced at them and could see some looking at him thoughtfully. Amira Hussein looked at him and then nodded approvingly at Duncan Lightfoot. Then she turned back to him.

"So, you believe that if he had been free to make his own decision he would have granted you the annulment?"

"I believe so, yes."

"On what grounds?"

"That the marriage was not lawful under God."

"But then we are back to where we started. You needed Catherine to lie. You needed her to say her first marriage to your brother was consummated."

"I believe he would have interpreted the passage in the bible as I did. It would have been enough for Catherine and Arthur to be married in sight of God to make it a legal marriage whether it was consummated or not."

"I think you are assuming a lot if you think any Pope would see it that way. It is my understanding that it was very difficult for a Catholic to get a divorce even fifty years ago. But you are telling me that 450 years ago a Pope would have granted you one just to suit your selfish desires. What kind of message would that have sent to the faithful?"

Henry paused before replying.

"It was an annulment not a divorce and the Pope could be a pragmatic man."

"You will have to explain that."

"The Protestant religion was taking hold across Europe. The Pope would not want a protracted dispute with England as this would encourage followers of the new religion here. I had been declared defender of the faith by the Pope so I believe he would have sided with me."

"You believed or Thomas Cromwell believed?"

"Cromwell was not my minister when I first asked for an annulment."

"But he was later. He was the one who came up with the plan to make you head of the Church of England bypassing Rome. Is that not true?"

"Yes,"

"I put it to you that when you first asked for an annulment it was all about your desire to marry Anne Boleyn. The more noble Charles the 5th angle only came later from the not inconsiderable brain of Thomas Cromwell. It was a justification for your behaviour rather than the real reason. Cromwell was what we now call a spin-doctor."

"I freely admit it was secondary but the fact that a foreign power had control over the Pope, and therefore England, had been a cause for concern long before my appeal for an annulment. The two issues are not unrelated. The Popes refusal of my request only highlighted the political problem."

"But even though it had been a cause for concern would you have split from Rome and set yourself up as head of the Church of England if you had had no desire to annul your marriage to Catherine? If the marriage had produced a son would you have split from Rome? If Anne Boleyn had never existed would you have done so?"

Henry felt the tension in the air. He looked at the jury who stared back at him expectantly. Amira Hussein looked relaxed and confident. She did not look unfriendly but Henry realised she was very dangerous. He looked at Lightfoot who nodded in a resigned kind of way.

"No. I would not have done so at that time."

He desperately wanted to say more but Lightfoot had cautioned against this. He remembered his advice.

"Say as little as possible Henry. Do not get drawn into arguments with her. This is what she wants, and she will lay traps for you. Give her as little to work with as possible. We will say what we want to say when I present the defence."

Now Amira Hussein turned to the jury again.

"So ladies and gentlemen of the jury, we have it from his own mouth. All the books, plays and movies were correct. Henry the 8th changed the religion of England to suit his own selfish desires. Millions of his subjects were plunged into terror as they were faced with either death for defying their King or being branded heretics for defying their Pope. He also cast aside, and imprisoned for the rest of her life, a good and noble woman who had loved and served him well."

Henry gripped the wooden bar in front of him. He wanted to explode. He opened his mouth to scream his protest but then forced his jaw closed as he looked at Lightfoot.

Amira Hussein smiled at him encouragingly.

"Was there something you wanted to add to that summary Henry?"

"You misrepresent me Madam."

She gave him a mocking smile.

"Really, how so?"

"My subjects were not plunged into terror and they did not become heretics. I did not change the religion of the country. That is a misunderstanding. All I did was claim the right to be head of the Church in England."

"Well that is your view and maybe your intention. But can you honestly say that many of your countrymen were not frightened by your break with the Pope?"

"They had no need to be and I believe them to be in the minority. Most were happy not to have a foreign power as head of the church."

"I find that doubtful but what about my other charge. Did you not imprison your first wife for the rest of her life?"

"She was kept well as befitted her station. She wanted for nothing."

"Well, nothing except freedom."

"We could have parted on good terms. If she had behaved better I would have given her more freedom. As it was she defied me for many years so I was not best pleased with her."

"When you say behaved better I assume you mean lie about how her first marriage was consummated?"

Henry hesitated as this was a difficult one. Lightfoot had told him what to say but it was true that he had asked Catherine to change her recollection of her first wedding night.

"It is true that I wanted her to say it had been consummated. When she refused to do so it put a strain on our relationship. But later I came to accept her refusal. But what I could not accept was her stubborn refusal to see that, if I was to provide an heir to the throne, our marriage had to end."

"So, you annulled the marriage and imprisoned her?"

"I put a limit on her activities. She lived in grand houses with servants. I would hardly call it a prison."

"Then I am not sure what your definition of a prison is. Mine, and I suspect everybody else's, would be where a person is not allowed to leave a building and was under guard. Did not both of these apply in the case of your wife?"

Henry was exasperated.

"This is preposterous. You have no understanding of the situation."

Amira Hussein nodded.

"Ok Henry, you are right. We only know what we read in history books. Please enlighten us to how it really was."

"The reality was that she refused to accept she was no longer my legal wife and my Queen. She refused to accept the split from Papal rule and she voiced these protests to all who would listen. I was aware of how popular she was with the people and that she could become a focal point for those who would protest against my new marriage and at the split from Rome. In short, if I had allowed her total freedom it could have encouraged rebellion in the country."

"Ok, and how did your cruel refusal to let her see her daughter fit into this plan to guard against rebellion. You even banned letters between them."

"Mary, like her mother, refused to accept that the marriage had been unlawful. She refused to accept Catherine was no longer Queen or my wife."

"As this would have made her a bastard I can see why. But come now Henry, isn't the real reason you kept them apart was that it caused misery to both? Despite what you say, most historians suggest that the accommodation you made both live in was decidedly uncomfortable."

"I offered both better accommodation, and more freedom, if they would recognise Anne Boleyn as Queen. Both refused."

"It was because they had principles Henry, something you seem to lack."

"You can insult me if you wish but I could not allow Catherine and Mary to protest so publicly about the change in religious thinking."

"So do you not accept in any way that your treatment of them both was both cruel and unworthy of a noble king?"

Henry thought about this. At Lightfoot's request he had been thinking about it a lot.

"I would accept that I was angry at Catherine's stubbornness. I wish now that I had made her final years more comfortable. But, for the reasons I have outlined, I cannot see how I could have managed things very differently. I do regret not trying to build a better relationship with Mary. But she was very close to her Mother, especially in her devotion to Rome and the Pope. She also shared her stubbornness."

"Do you not regret keeping them apart."

"I can see now, as I didn't then, how hurtful that was but there were valid reasons for doing so. Together they could have plotted against me."

"So you were scared of two women?"

"No, but I was aware of the support they had amongst my enemies."

"By enemies you mean those subjects who objected to your break with Rome?"

"Yes, but more so by the likes of Charles the 5th. He had sympathy for Catherine and was outraged by my split from the Pope."

Amira Hussein smiled.

"You see Henry, I do not buy it. Charles the 5th was not going to invade England to put his aunt Catherine on the throne and presumably execute you. He may have been angry at you but he wasn't going to go to war over it. No one was. At the time the major European powers and the Pope would have been hopeful of you returning England to the Roman fold. England was still essentially Catholic. You said it yourself. It wasn't like later when your daughter Elizabeth was the head of a protestant England. Then invasion was a real threat. But not in your time. Is that not true?"

"I was advised it was a real threat."

"Yes, by your spin-doctor Cromwell. But that was just to cover up the real reason. The truth is your treatment of Catherine and her daughter Mary was cruel, despicable and evil. You bullied Catherine and asked her to risk the wrath of her God to lie for you. When she refused you mentally tortured her. Out of sheer petulance you treated her abominably until her early death which I, and many others, believe you hastened. You Sir are a disgrace."

Henry glared at her. No one, not even his Father, had ever spoken to him so. Did he really have to take this from a mere woman?

"You know nothing woman. Catherine vexed me and continued to vex me but there were real political reasons why I treated her so."

"So it was not out of petulance that you did so? It wasn't out of sheer nastiness that you treated the woman who helped make you a true king so badly?"

"No it was not,"

The prosecutor smiled at him.

"So why, when you learnt of her death, did you have a celebration that lasted days? Why did you and Anne Boleyn wear yellow, the colour of rejoicing? Why did you wear a white feather in your cap and parade yours and Boleyn's daughter, Elizabeth, for all to see? Why did you tell courtiers to rejoice? And why Henry, if you were not petulant and cruel, did you deny Mary permission to attend her mother's death-bed or even her funeral? Is that not the definition of cruelty?"

Henry looked at her.

"You are correct in that I acted badly although you misinterpret many things. But you must realise that the death of Catherine allowed me and the country to move on. I could go on with my new marriage and as the head of the church. It ended the threat of war and allowed me to build bridges abroad. That is why I told my courtiers to rejoice."

"And your treatment of Mary, your daughter?"

Henry looked down for several seconds. Then he looked up and faced Amira Hussein.

"On that I have no defence. Not letting her attend her mother as she died as well as denying her a place at the funeral was indeed cruel."

Amira Hussein looked at him before turning to the judge.

"Your Honour, on this point the prosecution rests its case."

Chapter Nine

The case against Henry the 8th in regard to Catherine of Aragon
The Defence

"Henry, can you please tell me why your father wanted to make a marriage between you and Catherine of Aragon after your brother died and made her a widow?"

Henry smiled at Duncan Lightfoot's question.

"My father still wanted a political alliance with Aragon and Castille but the main reason was that he wanted to keep the large dowry that Catherine brought to the original marriage. In the terms of the contract, it should have been sent back to her father on Arthur's death."

"But you were just eleven years old and when Catherine's mother died before you could marry, she lost a lot of value in the political marriage stakes. Your father then advised you to withdraw and to break off the engagement. And this you did. Is that true?"

"My father did not give advice to his children, he gave orders. I had no wish to cancel the wedding contract."

"But when your father died and you became king the same political considerations still applied. You were only seventeen. I am sure you were advised by councillors that a better marriage, and consequently a better alliance with a European power, could be made."

"That is true."

"So Henry, I have a simple question for you. Why, in the face of strong opposition, did you marry Catherine of Aragon?"

"Because I loved her,"

"So it was that simple. You loved her."

"Yes,"

"And what was it about her that you loved?"

"I loved her spirit. After Arthur died my father kept her as a virtual prisoner and would not let her return home. She had little money but she never gave in to despair. She was made Spanish ambassador to England, the first female to ever hold that role. My father and his councillors thought they could bully her but she surprised them all. I had rarely seen anyone stand up to my father, especially a young woman. She was courageous and wise."

Lightfoot smiled.

"It is ironic that the virtues you loved in her at the beginning of your marriage would be the ones you hated when you came to end it. If she could stand up to your father's bullying she could stand up to yours."

"You are correct but I never envisaged ever wanting to end it."

"But at the start it was a love match and you were happy for many years."

"Yes, that is true."

"So when did the first problems come?"

Henry shrugged.

"There was only ever one problem. We never had a son. At first it did not matter but after many miscarriages I came to believe that God disapproved of the marriage."

"But this was many years into the marriage?"

"Yes, but obviously it became more urgent as Catherine approached an age when she could not conceive."

"But apart from this your relationship was still happy?"

"It put a strain on the marriage but relations were always cordial. I did not blame her for my lack of an heir. I just came to the conclusion that God would not allow us to have a male child. It says in the bible that if a man marries his brother's wife the couple would be childless."

"But, as my learned colleague pointed out, you did have a child."

"I took the bible quote to mean we would not have a son."

Lightfoot turned to look at the jury.

"And that is the crux of the matter ladies and gentlemen of the jury. We are here to judge Henry as a man not a king. But we cannot forget he was a king. For a man not to have a son is a disappointment. For a Tudor king not to have a son was a disaster. After many years of warfare Henry's father had triumphed in what we now call the war of the roses. But was the Tudor dynasty to end after just two generations? History has cast Henry as the villain and Catherine the wronged heroine. And I too admire Catherine but Henry's actions have to be seen in the context of his need to have a son."

He turned back to face Henry.

"Would you have divorced Catherine if you had had a son?"

"No,"

"But what of Anne Boleyn. Were you not in love with her?"

"No, I don't believe I was in love with her as I was with Catherine in the early days. She seduced and bewitched me but I would never have contemplated making her Queen if I had a son and heir."

"So she would have been a mistress as her sister Mary had once been?"

"Yes,"

"But that is not what most people take from the history books. The narrative in most depictions of your life is of you being completely under the spell of Anne Boleyn. It is said she denied you sex until you made her your Queen."

Amira Hussein stood up.

"I object to that my lord. The council for the defence is blurring the lines between factual and fictional accounts of the defendant's life."

Lightfoot looked at the judge.

"How can I not my lord? These events happened 450 years ago. While a lot of documents have survived, all of us are relying on the work of historians and many of them have contrary views on events. Also, my client is being judged by history and we all know history is changed by books and movies. The members of the jury have been heavily influenced by the almost uniformly negative depictions of Henry. I must be allowed to challenge those depictions."

The judge, a serious looking man of late middle-age, nodded.

"I agree. Objection denied."

Lightfoot turned back to Henry.

"So Henry, was it true? Did she deny you sex until you married her?"

"In the very beginning yes. Her uncle, the duke of Norfolk, sensed an opportunity when he knew Catherine was unlikely to have any more children. He advised his niece to hold out for marriage rather than a role as favoured mistress. But later it was me that held off as it was essential that any son I might have would be legitimate."

"If the Pope had agreed to your request to annul the marriage straight away what did you have planned for Catherine?"

"I wanted her to go into a nunnery but if she did not wish that I would have kept her in comfort somewhere."

"Would Catherine have accepted the annulment if the Pope had sanctioned it?"

"She would have hated it but she was devout in her faith and she would have abided by the Pope's wishes."

"So she would have acknowledged that Mary was illegitimate?"

"I very much doubt she would have acknowledged that publicly even if I had ordered it. But I would have spared her that."

"But Mary would officially be illegitimate or, more crudely, a bastard?"

"Yes, and that also caused me pain."

"Would you have made Catherine acknowledge Anne Boleyn as Queen? From what I have read of that lady I am pretty sure she would have insisted upon it."

Henry frowned.

"It is difficult but Catherine was very popular and that popularity among the people made them hate Anne. I would probably have had to insist upon it."

"And you did insist upon it and Catherine refused. Now I know that the Popes refusal to annul the marriage allowed Catherine to argue you were still married. But would she have acknowledged Anne if the Pope had annulled her marriage to you and gave his blessing to the one to Anne Boleyn?"

"No, I very much doubt it. Even for someone as devout as Catherine that would have been too much."

"Even if you had ordered her too?"

"I would have insisted to appease Anne but Catherine would rather have died than acknowledge Anne as my wife and Queen."

Lightfoot smiled.

"I can see why she was, and still is, so popular. So, if the Pope had granted you an annulment at the earliest stage you would have had sympathetic and warm feelings for Catherine? You would also have treated her as well as you could have even though she would have been very bitter towards you?"

"Yes, I would have,"

"But would you have kept her a prisoner even if it was a comfortable prison?"

"As long as she did not publicly condemn my new marriage or malign my new wife I would have allowed her as much freedom as was possible. And she would not have as it would have gone against the Pope's decree."

"As much freedom as possible, so she would still have had to ask your permission for certain things?"

"Yes as she would be living in houses provided by me and having her bills paid by me. But I would have placed very few restrictions on her as long as she did not plot against me."

"But of course none of this happened and, by denying that her first marriage was consummated, she made you wait over five years before you found a way to end your marriage."

"Yes,"

"And of course, this made you very bitter towards her?"

"Yes,"

"And until the day she died she still insisted she was the rightful Queen and she was still legally married to you? She also condemned your split from the Pope and refused to acknowledge Anne Boleyn as Queen?"

"Yes,"

"And for these reasons you kept a very tight rein on her. You could not allow her freedom as she would use that freedom to criticise you and the new Queen. She could also incite rebellion because of her devotion to the Catholic Church?"

"Yes. The Catholic powers of Europe, Spain and France, along with the emperor Charles the 5th had all condemned my actions and threatened invasion. I could not allow Catherine to become a flag-bearer for their cause."

"And is it not true that the reason you banned communication between Catherine and her daughter Mary was because you feared Mary would act as a messenger to Catherine's supporters."

"Yes, and I knew she would have."

Lightfoot turned towards the jury.

"So you see ladies and gentlemen of the jury, history has only told half the story. Bitter and vengeful Henry imprisoned Catherine and made her final years miserable. That is the narrative. But, while there was obviously a lot of personal spite, there were very valid reasons for doing so. Henry was King of England and he had a duty to keep the realm safe from invasion. Not allowing Catherine to go on a public campaign condemning him and his wife was a necessity. I would never blame Catherine for her fighting spirit but she had the power to change her circumstances. All she had to do was promise not to attack Henry, his wife or his decision to split from Rome."

"And then of course we come to that decision. The monumental decision that changed the religion of one of the most important countries in the world. For 12 hundred years England had been a Catholic country with the Pope in Rome at its head. And Henry changed all this just because he wanted a new wife. All of this is true, and Henry himself said the main reason was his desire to marry Anne. But it is not the whole truth."

"England did not suddenly become a protestant country the day Henry made himself head of the church of England, although this is what most movies and books about the episode imply. Protestants were still being burnt at the stake for heresy long afterwards. Henry still followed the Catholic faith and would to the day he died. He just wanted to be the ultimate power in that religion in a country in which he was King. And, as he has said to councillor for the prosecution, he wasn't taking that power from the Pope but Charles the 5th, the Holy Roman Emperor."

"Now I would urge you to ask yourself a question. How many of you had even heard of Charles the 5th let alone what part he played in one of the most important episodes in British history?"

"You see, when you mainly get your history from books and movies "Based on real events," you only get the abridged version. Hollywood movies are about 90 minutes long so they can only have so many characters and in this case Charles the 5th never makes the cut. Movies also have a formula-the good guys and the bad guys. The good guys are perfect in every sense while the villain is never allowed any redeeming characteristics. And in this case Catherine is the saintly heroine and Henry is the very bad guy."

"But real history is more nuanced than this. Henry undoubtedly treated his first wife very badly and his decision to split from Rome was selfish in the extreme. But there were also valid reasons why he acted as he did. Nothing is ever black and white where history is concerned and I would ask you to remember that as the trial continues."

He turned back to face Henry.

"Henry, was the colour yellow the celebration colour in your time? Was it the colour of joy?"

"Yes it was,"

"And did you and Anne Boleyn adorn yourself in yellow when you heard that Catherine had died? Did you and the court celebrate?"

Henry hesitated.

"Yes, we did."

"Why did you do that? It seems remarkably lacking in class."

"Her death was a relief in that it lifted the threat of invasion and I could get on with repairing my relationship with the European powers. Also, no one could any longer say that I was still legally wed to Catherine."

"So it was not done out of bitterness or spite? There was no hint of revenge on the woman who had fought you and foiled your plans for so long?"

Again, Henry hesitated. He and Lightfoot had rehearsed this but he still found it very hard.

"No, I can't in all honesty claim that."

"So it was done out of spite?"

"In part yes. Anne came up with the idea as she hated Catherine but I should not have allowed it."

"It has been suggested that yellow was the colour of mourning in Spain at the time."

Henry smiled.

"I would like that to be true as it would have put my actions in a more noble light. I was amused when I read it in a history book two days ago but it is unfortunately not true. The colour of mourning in Spain was black."

"Did you regret it?"

"Yes. When I was alone later, I remembered the early days of my marriage to Catherine and I cried. But it would not have been wise to grieve in public. It might have led to claims I regretted the split from Rome and my second marriage."

Lightfoot smiled.

"And at that point you did regret you marriage to Anne Boleyn didn't you?"

"Yes, but I didn't for one moment regret establishing the divine right of Kings."

Lightfoot again turned away from him.

"You see Ladies and gentlemen of the jury, Henry was a King but he had the same emotions as all other men. How can divorce proceedings that last for seven years not produce bitterness on both sides? Being King just complicated things and to a high degree. No one can say that he behaved well in this case but was he any different to millions of other men who dump their wives for a younger model? We don't send these men's souls to hell do we? Also on some points, such as the need to restrict her movements, he clearly felt he had no choice."

Lightfoot walked back to his desk and turned to the judge.

"Your honour that concludes the defence in the case of Catherine of Aragon."

"Thank you Mr Lightfoot. Miss Hussein, do you wish to cross-examine or make a comment to the jury in reply?"

She stood up.

"Yes, your honour,"

She walked to the front of her desk and looked at the jury.

"Ladies and Gentlemen of the jury I must congratulate my learned colleague on his re-invention of Henry the 8th. The despot with the volcanic temper is no more. The tyrant who executed all who failed him, even just one time after years of faithful service, was a myth. The homicidal maniac is gone and in his place is this calm reasonable man-not a King but a man who is humble enough to own up to his mistakes.

"But I am troubled. Cardinal Wolsey who tried and failed to get an annulment was accused of treason and would have been executed if he hadn't have died first. Sir Thomas More, who opposed both the second marriage and the split from Rome, ended up headless. There were numerous others as well. Anyone who openly opposed the marriage could find themselves accused of treason. So I fail to see how, as my learned colleague put it, Henry's divorce was like millions of other men's.

"No, I think this new reasonable Henry is the myth. I think that because these men were executed on Henry's orders and they can't be unexecuted. Their headless bodies are powerful testimony to the truth. The councillor for the defence can spin it any way he likes. He can, and probably will, argue that Wolsey, More and the others were guilty of other crimes but don't be fooled. It was the way Henry worked. There was never just one accusation. It covered up the selfish reasons for their demise."

She walked back to her desk and leaned back against it. Henry couldn't help thinking that she looked incredibly alluring. She looked at him as she spoke to the jury.

"No ladies and Gentlemen of the jury, do not be fooled. The Henry you read about is still the real Henry."

She turned to the judge.

"That is all I wish to say on this matter My Lord. "

"Well, I think that is a good time to finish for the day," said the judge. "We will resume at 9 tomorrow morning but for now the court is adjourned."

Chapter Ten

"Why was she allowed to say that. It was a lie. Wolsey was secretly trying to get Anne Boleyn exiled. He was working against me. He was also corrupt and had made himself rich. And More openly challenged my right to be head of the Church. It had nothing to do with me marrying Anne Boleyn. Why did you not challenge her on this?"

"Because it would have been counterproductive. She was right. The accusation of Wolsey working secretly behind your back is doubtful at best. He almost certainly used his position to enrich himself but that was true of all your inner circle. It is true of most people in powerful positions. It never bothered you when he was successfully doing your bidding. No, the real reason he was accused of treason was because he failed to get you an annulment."

"That's not true,"

"Yes, it is true Henry so please stop fooling yourself and admit it. Thomas More was executed for religious reasons but those reasons only existed because of your desire to wed again. It was ultimately about Anne Boleyn. It was always about Anne Boleyn at that time."

Henry sighed.

"Will I never be rid of her?"

"No, probably not. But don't be despondent as it went well in there and you did very well."

"Do you really think so? Didn't her last statement damage me?"

"A little but this was never going to be easy. Amira is a very formidable opponent."

"You make it sound like a game."

Lightfoot smiled.

"It is a game but it is one we are both desperate to win."

"But you don't face any consequences if you lose, not compared to me anyway."

"That's true,"

"So my fate depends on who is the better lawyer, you or her."

"God, I hope not as we would be buggered. She is much better than me. But even the best get beaten sometimes. And more than anything it depends on you Henry and how you conduct yourself in court."

"Why should that matter so much?"

"It is quite simple. If people like you they are less likely to send your soul to hell."

"But it is not that simple is it? If they judge me to be guilty of all I am accused of surely they would have no choice."

"Yes, that is true but that is another reason you have to stay calm. You have to answer all questions very carefully. If you get in a self-entitled rage you will say something you will regret for a very long time. "

"But all this is ridiculous. I was the only live witness to these events. But that girl and the jury prefer to doubt me and believe the lies that have been told for centuries."

"You are right. It is ridiculous and unfair but that can change. If the Henry in that courtroom is not the same as all of the portrayals of you they will start to question what else they have been told."

Henry frowned.

"It seems a very weak strategy. Do you not have any other plans?"

Lightfoot smiled.

"Possibly,"

"But you are not going to tell me what they are? That hardly seems fair. It is my soul that is in danger."

"True but I don't want to confuse the issue. I want you to concentrate on answering the questions, in the way we are going to discuss, in a calm measured way."

"How do you know what questions they will ask?"

Again, Lightfoot smiled.

"There are not many advantages in defending a man after he has been found guilty a million times in the court of public opinion. But one is that everyone knows what questions are going to be asked."

Chapter Eleven

The case Against Henry the 8th in regard to Anne Boleyn

The Prosecution

"When did you tire of Anne Boleyn Henry?"

He looked at her, somewhat surprised by her opening attack.

"Within two years I knew the marriage was wrong,"

"That is an interesting choice of words. Do you mean it was a mistake?"

"It was a mistake on my part in that I did not recognise her true character. It was wrong in the same way my marriage to Catherine was wrong. I had bedded her sister before her."

Amira Hussein laughed.

"Oh, come now Henry that sounds very weak. You are comparing your brother's marriage to Catherine with a tawdry affair?"

Henry felt his face redden. Cromwell had made the same point many years before. But Cromwell had also come up with the idea and declared it valid.

"In the eyes of God the sin was the same."

"And that is how you justified the annulment of your marriage to Anne Boleyn?"

"It was true, no matter how much you mock,"

"And of course this time you had no trouble getting the annulment as you were the head of the Church. You really are a piece of work Henry."

"The Archbishop of Canterbury decided the issue, not me."

"Please do not insult our intelligence Henry. Cranmer did your bidding. Everyone at that time did your bidding. So why wasn't that enough? If you had annulled the marriage, why did she have to die?"

"She was found guilty of treason, treasonable adultery and witchcraft."

"So it had nothing to do with the fact she had just miscarried a male baby?"

"No, I was angry at that but that was not the reason."

"You were angry at that! Do you not mean you were angry with her? You were heard saying that she had betrayed you."

Henry paused before answering.

"It is true. I was angry with her. I know how cruel that looks now but you have to realise that a King has to have a son. It is the first and foremost requirement. People must remember this when it comes to judging my actions."

"Oh, I could consider that Henry. I could excuse your heartless anger if two months later you hadn't chopped her head off. Are we meant to put that down to your disappointment at not having a son? Are we meant to forgive you killing your wife, a minstrel with limited intelligence and four of your best friends because you were so deeply hurt by Anne's failure?"

Henry felt his anger rise.

"That is not how it was."

"Really? So please enlighten us to how it was Henry."

"I was given reports that my wife may have committed adultery. I ordered my first minister, Thomas Cromwell, to investigate those reports. He discovered there was substance to the intelligence as well as possible treason and witchcraft. Those concerned were arrested, tried, found guilty and executed."

"Just like that? There was less than twenty days between their arrests and execution. Are we really meant to believe that a thorough investigation and then a trial can be held in that time?"

"All proper procedures were followed."

"The day after Anne Boleyn's execution you became engaged to Jane Seymour. Is that correct?"

"Yes,"

"And ten days later you were married?"

"Yes,"

"So it would seem rather convenient timing that your second wife suddenly became a treasonous adulterer and witch. I suppose that is just coincidence. Would that be a correct assumption?"

"It would appear that her crimes had been going on for some time."

"What was the evidence against Henry Norris?"

"A conversation between them was overheard,"

"Yes, as I understand it one of her ladies in waiting told how Anne had accused Norris of coming to her chambers not to pay court to Madge Shelton, another lady in waiting, but Anne herself. It was also reported that the Queen welcomed this attention. Is this true?"

"Yes, I believe it was part of the prosecution case."

"And Anne was overheard suggesting to another of her alleged lovers that, and I quote, "He would want to fill another man's shoes if that were possible." This was interpreted by the court as them discussing your death. Is that correct?"

"Yes. To imagine the King's death is to wish the King's death. It is treason."

"Yes, but what I find baffling is that every single conversation she ever had appeared to be overheard but no one seemed to notice her having sex with five different men. Can you explain that to me?"

Henry paused, knowing how unlikely it sounded.

"I can't explain it."

"Well,, I think I can and I think the jury can. I think anyone who has read of this in the last 450 years can explain it. The explanation is that she did not have sex with five different men. The explanation is that they were trumped up charges so she could be executed and you would be free to marry Jane Seymour."

"I do not believe that to be the case."

"Why not?"

"I trusted my councillors and the court."

"And so, when they said her and some of your best friends were guilty of adultery and treason you just accepted that?"

"How could I not. How could I undermine the law."

Amira Hussein laughed.

"You really are a card, Henry. You wanted them found guilty and no one was going to go against that wish. Do not take me or the jury for fools Henry. We are not your lackeys. Is it not true that the evidence was incredibly weak. Can you not admit even that?"

"I did not interfere with the court proceedings."

"This is one of the charges against Henry Norris and the Queen. In October 1533 Anne was accused of "Procuring" Norris to "Violate" her at Westminster. At that time Anne was still confined to her chambers at Greenwich after giving birth to her daughter Elizabeth. In 1535 the Queen was actually at Richmond when she was charged with having sex with Mark Smeaton at Greenwich. The people who framed them didn't even bother to work too hard as they knew the verdict was a foregone conclusion. These dates were easily checked but no one bothered. A defence lawyer would have done so but you weren't going to let them have one of them were you?"

"I have no answer to that as I didn't oversee the investigation. But I do believe there was a line in the charge about various other times both before and after those dates."

"Oh yes, there would be but any fair-minded person would not consider "Various other times" as a basis for execution. The truth was that there was hardly any evidence against them and what little there was could easily be disproved. Is that not the case?"

"No,"

"Henry, Mark Smeaton confessed to having sex with the Queen at Greenwich when we now know for certain that Anne was at Richmond at the time. Does this not prove that the confession, that was almost certainly elicited by torture, was false?"

"No, it does not and I don't know if he was tortured."

"Did you ask if he was?"

"No, as it was not my place to."

"How convenient. See no evil hear no evil. Is it not true that you didn't ask because you didn't want to know the truth. Is this not what you always did. If you didn't ask how Cromwell and others delivered what you wanted you couldn't be blamed for it. Your stock answer is that the law was followed at all time. Is that not you ducking responsibility for the deaths of people you knew were probably innocent?"

"No, that is not the case. It was not for me to interfere with the judicial process."

"Henry, answer me honestly. Do you think all those men had sex with Anne Boleyn?"

Henry thought about his answer carefully.

"If you had seen them round her you would not be so sure they didn't."

"Henry, that is not an answer. Please answer the question."

"I think it is unlikely that she had sex with all of them because of the risk of discovery. But I don't doubt they would have done if they could. That to me constitutes adultery and, even worse, a conspiracy to end my life."

She looked surprised. It was what he had long believed but he had never said as much. He wouldn't have done so here if Lightfoot had not suggested that it would be a good move.

"You think they were plotting your death?"

"I believe Anne Boleyn, and her family, were desperate for a male child. She could have tried to pass him off as my own. This is especially true of George Boleyn, her brother. This would be treason of the highest order."

"Oh, come now Henry. George Boleyn was added to the list of suspects just because he was on the privy council. It would have been awkward to say the least to have him there after you had killed his sister."

"You didn't see them together. They were always more like lovers than siblings. And Anne, and even more so her uncle, the Duke of Norfolk, would have thought nothing of passing off a child created out of incest as mine."

"Do you really believe all this?"

"Yes,"

"And who first suggested this to you?"

Henry hesitated and Amira Hussein smiled.

"I think we already know the answer don't we Henry. It was Thomas Cromwell, wasn't it?"

"Yes, it was Cromwell but what he said made sense."

"He always did make sense, didn't he? Right up to the point he displeased you and you had him executed."

Henry was about to answer but Lightfoot intervened.

"Your honour, I object. The Cromwell execution is a separate part of the prosecution's case."

Amira Hussein smiled.

"I think Mr. Lightfoot fears his client may go off script your honour."

"Perhaps, but the objection is sustained. Do not get ahead of yourself Ms Hussein."

"So Henry, Cromwell had come up with a plan on how you could end your marriage to Catherine and he did the same to end the one with Anne. Is that not true?"

"I had asked him and Cranmer to explore the possibility of an annulment but that is all. When I heard the rumours of adultery and treason I got Cromwell to investigate."

She smiled.

"And did you do so in a way that he could interpret as you wanting the accusations to be true?"

Henry hesitated.

"I was not aware of doing so but it is possible he got this impression."

"Oh, it think it more than a possibility Henry. I am pretty sure probability doesn't even cover it. I suggest to you that Cromwell left that meeting thinking he was pretty much under orders to find Anne guilty. And this would have suited him would it not? Just weeks before she had criticised his domestic and foreign policies in your presence. If you had taken her side it could have cost him his life. She was now a danger to him wasn't she? "

"I asked him to investigate. That is all."

"And his investigation freed you up to marry Jane Seymour and for Cromwell to rid himself of some enemies at court. How very convenient for both of you."

Henry looked at her before speaking very calmly.

"Your view on these proceedings is very wrong. History's view on these proceedings is very wrong."

"Well, I think we will let the jury decide on that one. What was your reaction when you first heard that Anne may have committed adultery?"

Henry was surprised by the question and the change of tack.

"Well, I was outraged of course,"

"But you said earlier that they might have only talked about having an affair because of the risk of discovery if they actually did have sex."

"I think that may have been the case but I would argue they were still having an affair, as you put it, but without the physical act."

"But it wasn't adultery in the literal sense?"

"That may have been the case."

"So it wasn't like the adultery you practised many times in all your many marriages, especially the first two?"

Henry was stunned.

"But...But.."

"But what Henry?"

"But that is very different. That was not adultery."

"Henry, you were married and you had sex with other women. Many of those women were married. Please explain to me and the jury how, even in your times, that is not adultery?"

"Well, it is different... It is not the same."

"So it is alright for you to sleep with countless women but it is not alright for your wives to do the same."

"No, of course not. It is a different situation."

"Please explain why it is different because I must confess I am baffled. I am pretty sure the jury is as well."

"I was the King."

Amira Hussein smiled in triumph.

"So, there we have it from your own mouth. You were the King and normal rules of decent behaviour did not apply to you. Did you never consider the thoughts of the husbands of these women, some of whom were your friends, when you took their wives as a Mistress. Did you never consider the thoughts of the women or your own wives?"

Henry really hadn't.

"The times were vastly different. Every King in Christendom took Mistresses."

"A strange contradiction in terms when you consider one of the ten commandments says you shall not commit adultery or covet another man's wife. You really were a pig of a man weren't you Henry."

Lightfoot stood up but the judge was quicker.

"Miss Hussein, you do discredit to your profession when you stoop to insults. I will have no more of it. You shall withdraw the remark."

"I was just making the point that Henry's behaviour was contemptible your honour. I accept I went too far but this court is here to assess the defendants behaviour above all else. I believe it is so evil that it deserves the ultimate sanction. I feel I should be allowed to make my case. Henry is accused of a lot worse crimes than adultery on a grand scale but it does highlight how unfeeling he was to other people. And he carried this lack of empathy onto his future dealing with his wives and others."

"I take your point and I accept it. But I must insist you rephrase the remark."

She nodded.

"Thank you, your honour and I will do so gladly."

She turned slightly and smiled at Henry.

"You really weren't a very nice man were you Henry?"

Henry felt his face redden as the jury laughed. No one, let alone a woman had ever dared mock him so. He gripped the rail in front of him as his temper flared.

"I am the King of England. How dare you, a mere woman, speak to me like that?"

"I dare because you are not King here. I dare because here women are not men's plaything's to be bartered off in marriage, cheated on and abandoned, or in your case, executed when they are no longer any use. I dare because here women don't have to be scared of evil, selfish tyrants."

"I was not a tyrant. I was a just King."

"Well again, I think the jury will decide on that. In this court you benefit from the modern belief that the accused is innocent until proven guilty.   Is it not true Henry that in your time the onus was on the accused to prove their innocence?"

"That is broadly the case but it was not something I brought in. It had been the way for years."

"But Anne Boleyn and her alleged lovers were not given any chance to prove their innocence. They had no legal representation and no time to build a defence. They didn't even really know what they were being charged with until they got to the court. This was not justice. It was murder. Is that not the case."

"No, the trials were fair as far as I know. I did not conduct them and I wasn't even there."

"What nonsense. You might not have been physically there but your instructions certainly were. Everyone in those courts, especially the judges, knew their duty. It was a sham and the verdicts a foregone conclusion. Can you not admit that?"

Henry paused.

"I believe that they were more likely to be guilty than not guilty. But I gave no instructions."

"So, if they had been found not guilty what would have changed? Would you have stayed married to Anne Boleyn? Would you have stayed with her even though you had come to despise her and think her a witch? Would you have stayed married to her even if she never gave you a son?"

Henry looked at her a long time before giving his answer.

"No, I wouldn't have stayed married to her."

Amira Hussein gave a half-smile and turned to the judge.

"No further questions My Lord."

Chapter Twelve

The case against Henry the 8th in regard to Anne Boleyn

The Defence

"Ladies and Gentlemen of the jury I would like you to open your minds. I want you to consider something that has very rarely been considered in 450 years. No Hollywood producer has done so and pretty much no novelist. Even esteemed historians do not give it much consideration. But I want you to consider it. What if Anne Boleyn, and the men executed with her, were guilty as charged?"

Lightfoot walked along beside the bench, making eye contact with every juror, before walking back to the centre of the room. Henry was impressed with the man's ability to hold everyone's attention. It was almost regal.

"Of course it is an outlandish idea. Everyone knows they were trumped up charges and the verdicts a foregone conclusion. Every book, movie or TV documentary has told us that. They can't all be wrong can they? Well, yes, I think it is possible that they are."

Now he walked slowly across the room and the eyes of the jury followed his every move.

"You see, no one questions the traditional narrative because it is so embedded. For over 450 years it has become so accepted no one even thinks to challenge it. There are not many certainties in history, but this has become one. Henry the 8th wanted rid of Anne Boleyn so he, and his minister Cromwell, trumped up some charges and had their heads cut off. But I am going to challenge that certainty and I want you to give due consideration to that challenge."

He walked back and faced Henry.

"Henry, were you good friends with Sir Henry Norris, Sir Francis Weston and Sir William Brereton?"

"Yes, I had known them for many years."

"Were they enemies of Thomas Cromwell?"

"Most, if not all my court, hated Cromwell.

"Why was that?"

"He was not of their class. He was the son of a blacksmith and many in the court thought him an upstart. They were also jealous because he had my ear and I had promoted him to high office. They were also scared of him of course."

"What was your relationship with him?"

"I liked him well enough and he was brilliant at solving problems."

"Were you friends?"

"No. He was just my chief minister."

"So, you were not friends in the way you were with Norris, Weston and Brereton?"

"No, of course not. They were friend from back when I was a youth."

"Tell me the truth. Did you too look down on Cromwell because of his low birth?"

Henry thought about it.

"I valued him highly but I suppose I was always aware that he was not of the nobility."

"Do you think it is possible that the council for the prosecution is right? Could Cromwell have falsely accused Norris, Weston, and Brereton because they were enemies and he wanted rid of them."

"I find that highly unlikely. If this had been his intention he would have chosen far worse enemies. These three were little threat to him."

"Why would that be? Did you not listen to their views?"

"Yes, but they did not hold high office. They were not involved with policy."

"Did they ever speak ill of Cromwell to you?"

"Everyone spoke ill of Cromwell."

"And, as we will see later in the trial, you eventually succumbed to this pressure from the nobility and turned on Cromwell. Is that not true?"

"I regret to say that it is true. Cromwell was not innocent and had clearly abused his position. But he had served me and the country well and I should have been lenient with him. But the noble members of my council, led by the Duke of Norfolk, persuaded me that his crimes were worthy of execution and, because I was displeased with him at the time, I agreed."

Lightfoot turned to look at the jury.

"You see Ladies and Gentlemen of the jury, I find that interesting. The events Henry describes take place in 1540. At that stage Cromwell was very powerful but even then he would have been aware of how fragile his position was. His many enemies were also powerful and many were close personal friends with the King. They were also of his class. Cromwell was always the outsider."

Lightfoot looked at Henry and then walked across to the jury looking thoughtful.

"Now, considering that, how much more fragile was his position in 1536? He had the same powerful enemies but he was relatively new to the post of chief minister. He had helped the King get his divorce from Catherine but he had not yet built up a store of credit. One wrong move could result in his downfall which, given his enemies, would mean execution."

He again looked thoughtful before continuing.

"Now, knowing this would he really have falsely accused three of Henry's closest friends? Surely he would have known the consequences if Henry refused to accept this or it was proven the accusation was false. Would Thomas Cromwell, one of the smartest and canniest men in history, have taken such a risk? I don't think so."

Henry saw several members of the jury look at each other and nod in silent agreement.

"Which of course leads us to the conclusion that Cromwell felt safe in informing the King that the three men had been implicated in possible adultery and treason. He felt safe because he had solid evidence. He felt safe because he at least suspected that they were guilty."

Lightfoot turned towards Henry.

"Do you think Cromwell would have lied to you on this matter Henry?"

"No I do not,"

"Were you shocked?"

"Yes, of course. But then I thought about how they were around her. They were completely under her spell and then the accusations did not seem unrealistic."

"Now, and be completely honest here Henry, did you not also feel a certain excitement at the news as you knew this could lead to the quick end of your marriage?"

"I can't deny that the thought came to me."

"And Cromwell would also have known this?"

"Yes,"

"But that does not mean that they were innocent does it?"

"No. Both Cromwell and I thought there was substance to the accusation."

"Did you ever have a conversation with Cromwell about ensuring a guilty verdict?"

"No,"

"I have another question, Henry. What if it had just been one of them, along with the Queen, who had been found guilty of the same crimes? Would the result have been the same. Would they both have been executed?"

"Yes,"

Lightfoot turned towards the jury.

"You see Ladies and gentlemen of the jury, that has always been something that has bothered me about the accepted trumped-up charges theory. Why were five men falsely accused and found guilty? What was the point when one would have served the same purpose? If It was dangerous for Cromell to falsely accuse members of the nobility he could have just stuck with the first of the accused. Mark Smeaton was just a musician, a court minstrel. Cromwell could have accused him with no danger to himself."

Lightfoot walked along the bench again. Henry could see it was a tactic of his to get as close to the jury as possible. His aim was to build up an affinity with them and make them feel he was one of them.

"Now, I can see that this might not be quite enough. It would possibly be untidy and people might question if a Queen of good birth would really have sex with a lowly servant. So, if you believe the false charges theory, maybe a member of the nobility was required. But why three, along with George Boleyn, Anne's brother, when one would have done?"

Lightfoot paused and made eye contact with a middle aged lady on the front row of the jury.

"So now we have to question why Cromwell would do so. Why did he accuse five men when one, or maybe two, would have done? And why, again if we believe the accepted theory, did the King go along with it. And when we come up with the inevitable answer that both believed there was substance to the charges we have to question that very theory. Maybe the men, and Anne Boleyn, were guilty. And, even if we can't bring ourselves to ditch 450 years of propaganda, surely we can consider that Cromwell and the King genuinely thought they might be guilty."

Again Henry was pleased to see several members of the jury nod in agreement. Lightfoot turned towards Henry.

"Henry, prior to hearing these charges how were you planning to end your marriage to Anne Boleyn?"

"I was going to seek an annulment."

"On what grounds?"

"On the grounds that I had previously bedded her sister, Mary."

"So basically it was the same grounds as in your previous annulment to Catherine except you had not married Mary?"

"That is correct ."

"Even to me it seems a little weak Henry. The quote in the bible that you used in the Catherine annulment specifically mentions marriage. It makes no mention of it being against God's law to marry the sister of a woman you had once bedded."

Henry frowned. He had had the same objection from Cranmer.

"I believe it is open to interpretation."

"But do you agree that it is weak. I am sure your ministers thought so."

Henry reluctantly nodded.

"Yes, it was weak."

"But you could have pushed it through couldn't you. Ultimately you were now head of the church in England. You no longer had to beg the Pope for an annulment."

"Yes, I could have."

"So why didn't you?"

"It was a last resort. Cromwell and Cranmer thought it would damage the new church of England. I still followed the doctrines of the Roman church even though I recognised the supremacy of Kings."

"So what were the other alternatives?"

"I could declare that the marriage was illegal."

Lightfoot smiled.

"But that would automatically mean you were still legally wed to Catherine. Is that not true?"

"Yes,"

"Now, I can understand why you would not want to do this up to 1536. But on January the 8th Catherine died. Could you not then have had Cranmer declare that the marriage to Anne Boleyn was illegal and you were still legally married to Catherine?"

"Yes,"

"And of course you were now a widower and free to marry Jane Seymour?"

"Yes, that is correct."

"So why didn't you?"

"Cranmer did eventually declare it illegal."

"Yes, but only two days before Anne's execution. Why did you not order him to do so before? Why did you not choose this path to end the marriage? Surely it would have been easier. No one needed to die, not Anne or your friends?"

"That was what I was going to do."

"So why didn't you?"

Henry paused and looked at the jury before answering.

"Because, before we could do so we received evidence of adultery, treason, witchcraft and incest."

Lightfoot smiled and then walked towards the jury.

"You see Ladies and Gentlemen of the jury, this is another thing the movies, the authors and even the historians leave out. There was absolutely no need to invent charges against Anne Boleyn and the others. Anne could have returned to the bosom of her very rich family and Norris and the others could have remained as valued courtiers. With Catherine dead all Henry had to do was declare his second marriage illegal. Then he was free, under the rules of every church, to marry again."

He again made eye contact with the same lady.

"Could it be that the reason he didn't take this much easier course is this- He was convinced that there was substance to the allegations and that they should be investigated. Maybe, and this goes against all you have learnt, Anne Boleyn was not executed because she was an impediment to Henry's plan to marry Jane Seymour. We now know that was not true. Maybe she was just executed because a court found her guilty as charged."

He walked back to his desk and looked at the judge.

"This concludes the defence in regard to Anne Boleyn my lord."

"Thank you Mr. Lightfoot. Miss Hussein, do you wish to cross-examine?"

"Yes, your honour I do have a few questions,"

She stood up and looked at Henry thoughtfully.

"Henry, I want some clarification. Have I got this timeline broadly right? Rumours came to you that a lady-in waiting to Queen Anne had made allegations against her. She had suggested she had behaved inappropriately with several men. She had even hinted at adultery. Is that correct?"

"I heard the rumours, yes."

"And you then asked Cromwell to investigate?"

"Yes,"

"And one of the first people he questioned was the musician Mark Smeaton. He was detained by Cromwell at his house and he confessed to adultery with the Queen and named the others who would eventually be executed?"

"Yes,"

"And Cromwell brought that signed confession to you?"

"Yes,"

"You see, I find that interesting because Mr. Lightfoot has highlighted that Cromwell would not make a false allegation against your long-time friends. I agree with him when he says there is no way he would take the risk. I agree with him that such a clever man as Cromwell would know his life would be forfeit if you rejected the allegations. But Cromwell did not do that. What Cromwell did was bring you a signed confession. He made no allegation of his own. Is that correct?"

"Yes,"

"And you of course could not reject the confession even if it implicated your friends could you?"

"No, of course not,"

"And of course you had no wish to did you? After all you must have known the confession in your hand practically guaranteed the end of your marriage."

"I cannot deny that the thought came to me but I was shocked by the confession."

"But not shocked enough to enquire of Cromwell if he had obtained the confession by torture?"

"I was not in the habit of questioning the methods of my ministers."

"No, of course you weren't as you didn't want to entertain any doubt that the confession was genuine. Do you truly believe that torture wasn't used on Smeaton?"

"I don't know but I suspect not."

"Why? Most historians are convinced it was. It was not unusual at the time, was it? Suspects were often tortured to confess to whatever the interrogator wanted them to. Is that not true?"

"Yes, it was but, while Cromwell was capable of being brutal, he was intelligent and subtle enough to get the truth out of a man like Smeaton. I should also point out that Smeaton never retracted his confession even on the scaffold."

"You make a good point Henry but maybe he did this because Cromwell threatened the lives of his family if he did so?"

Lightfoot stood up.

"Objection my Lord. This is pure guess work. There is absolutely no evidence for this allegation in any history book."

"I agree and the jury will disregard the remark. Miss Hussein, please stick to, if not the known facts, at least the known theories."

She nodded.

"My apologies my Lord. Ok Henry I accept your point although I still believe it more likely that Cromwell obtained the confession through torture. Is it not also true that, by the convention of the time, noblemen such as Norris could not be tortured while commoners such as Smeaton could be?"

"That is true."

"So that probably explains why Cromwell detained him first doesn't it?"

"I have no comment to make on that."

"No, I bet you haven't. But can we agree that by Cromwell bringing to you the confession he was not risking his life?"

Henry thought about it.

"No, I do not agree. There was less danger than if he had made a straight allegation. But he would not know my reaction. If I had immediately suspected his methods of obtaining the confession I might have rejected it and questioned his motives."

"But then you would still have the problem of being married to Anne."

"Yes,"

" So you weren't ever going to question it were you?

"Probably not."

"And Cromwell would know this?"

"He would have suspected as much."

"So, as has been said before, it was very convenient for both of you. You got an annulment and Cromell rid himself of some enemies."

"I have answered that question before. Cromwell had far worse enemies and we both believed there was substance to the allegations."

"But did Anne criticise his domestic and foreign policies?"

"Yes, as did many others."

"But at that stage you were pretty fed up with Anne Boleyn weren't you. Her intelligence and irreverent wit were very appealing in a mistress but less so in a wife. Is that fair?"

"I would not have expressed it so but you are probably right. She got mixed up in affairs that were not her business."

"So Cromwell had nothing to fear from her did he?"

"No,"

"But what if she had produced a son. Surely that would have changed everything. Her stock would rise in your eyes. Surely then Cromwell might worry about her criticising him and even questioning his loyalty to you. Is that not the case?"

"I cannot imagine ever taking her side against Cromwell in matters of state."

"But your record, especially in the later part of your reign, suggests you did take some very questionable advice from unqualified people. You would eventually take other people's side against Cromwell and this would lead to his execution. Is that not true?"

"It is not the same thing. I got false information about Cromwell and in a weak moment I believed it. But the men who gave it to me were not unqualified. They were members of the privy council."

"But Cromwell would have known the danger if relations between you and Anne improved. Would you not agree that he was a man who could see danger from a long way away?"

"I would agree that he had remarkable foresight."

"And would you also agree that he normally found ways of neutralising any potential threat?"

"I would agree but I very much doubt he saw Anne as a threat."

"I beg to differ Henry. You had fallen under this woman's spell before. If she produced a male heir you may have fallen under it again. You had changed the religion of England for this woman. You had risked war with Spain, France and the Holy Roman Empire. Cromwell would know that if you were again enamoured by Anne his life would be forfeit. So he had to get rid of her and when you expressed a desire to end the marriage he saw his opportunity. Is that not exactly what happened?"

"No, I do not think so and if he had done so why, as my council has said, did he need to accuse five men. One would have done."

"That is an interesting question. Mr. Lightfoot thinks it unlikely but I am not so sure. We sort of agree that the commoner Mark Smeaton would not be enough. Cromwell needed a member of the nobility but why three, four if you include George Boleyn?" Were Norris, Weston and Brereton especially close to the Queen? Were they prominent members of her inner circle?"

Henry smirked.

"They were like bees round a honeypot. Norfolk and the others used to joke about it. As I said, they were under her spell."

"And you mean that, don't you? It is not like modern times when we use the term loosely as we know witches don't exist. In your time witches were real. And you believe you were bewitched by Anne when you married her and so were Norris, Weston and Brereton. Is that the case?"

"Yes,"

"Do you believe most of your subjects accepted this explanation? Did most of the nobles?"

"I believe so, yes,"

"She was not popular was she, either with the people or with the nobles?"

"No. Catherine had been very popular with the people and many blamed Anne for her downfall. Also, she made enemies at court with her high-handed ways."

"Do you believe Cromwell thought she was a real witch?"

Henry paused as he considered this.

"I doubt it. He was a very practical man."

"I agree and I don't think you really believed it either Henry, not deep down. I also think many others would have doubts. Cynicism was not unknown in your time-in fact it was very prominent. But, after causing the biggest upheaval in religious history and then annulling the marriage to the woman who was the reason for that upheaval, cynicism may have turned to anger and even rebellion. Is that not a possibility?"

"It is possible but doubtful."

"I am sure Cromwell saw it as more than a slight possibility and I suspect he conveyed this concern to you. No, you had to make the charges against her so obscene and vile that no one could doubt that she was a witch. So one, or even two, were not enough. People associate witches with sexual depravity so you made her as big a whore as possible. You even claimed she practiced incest with her own brother. This way there would be no anger and no rebellion. Is this not the case?"

"No, of course not,"

"Did Cromwell consider this path?"

Henry hesitated.

"I very much doubt it but, If he did he did, he did not mention it to me."

She gave a scornful laugh.

"Oh, I believe that alright. It was not how it worked was it? You gave your instructions much more subtlety."

"I gave no such orders in any way."

"Yes you did Henry, not in so many words but you did. You gave Cromwell free rein to end your marriage in such a way that no blame could attach to you. When you told Cromwell that you believed Anne was a witch it was your way of ordering him to make everyone else believe it. And he did just that didn't he?"

"No. If Cromwell got that impression, and I doubt he did, it was not my intent."

"No Henry, that will not do. Let us be clear. Cromwell is not on trial here, you are. Cromwell almost certainly had his own agenda but he would not have gone against your wishes. Anne and the others would not have died if you had not wished it."

"For God's sake woman, I did not wish the death of my friends. There were allegations of treason and these allegations were investigated. They were found guilty and they paid the only possible penalty for treason. Why do you not accept that this scenario is much more likely than your wild theories."

"Because it is too convenient for you Henry."

"That does not make it untrue. As Lightfoot said, why didn't I just annul the marriage after Catherine died and banish Anne from court? There was no need to fake charges against her."

Amira Hussein nodded thoughtfully and walked a small circle in the court room.

"You do make a valid point Henry but I think there are a quite a few reasons. One would be Cromwell's fear that she, or her family, could damage him."

Henry snorted his disgust.

"You are really struggling now aren't you? If Anne was of little danger to him as my Queen it would be non-existent after she had fallen from favour and banished from court."

"But her uncle, the Duke of Norfolk, would have been a danger to him. Was he not Cromwell's bitterest rival?

"Norfolk fell from my favour for a long time after Anne's execution. He had pushed me to marry his niece in an effort to improve his own position at court."

"And his position had improved hadn't it? Following your marriage to Anne, Norfolk had risen to a very powerful position. Only Cromwell was higher. Is that not the case?"

"Yes,"

"And after Anne's fall, he lost a lot of that power."

"I stripped him of no honours or duties. He kept his position."

"Yes, you did but everyone was aware he was out of favour. He was rarely given a private audience with you and he was, to a certain extent, side-lined. Would you agree with that?"

"Yes, I did not speak to him for months."

"So his standing went down after Anne's execution and Cromwell's went up."

Henry paused. He had to remember Lightfoot's warning that this woman was very clever. He nodded.

"Yes,"

She smiled.

"So would that not be a reason for Cromwell to massively exaggerate his niece's crimes? Would this incredibly clever man who, as you say, had remarkable foresight, not see this as a great opportunity to damage his chief rival at court?"

Henry again hesitated as he remembered the two men's mutual dislike.

"The second part of your statement is undoubtedly true. He would have seen the possibilities in the charges and how they could benefit him. But that does not mean he faked those charges."

"But you would agree that this could be a reason why Anne was executed, after the most vile accusations, rather than just divorced."

Henry nodded slowly.

"It would be a reason if you were so determined to disbelieve the truth that Anne was guilty of the crimes she was accused of."

Amira Hussein smiled.

"Ok Henry, we have established one reason now may I be permitted to advance another?"

Henry sighed in contempt.

"If you must,"

"Thank you Henry. Now, I do believe Cromwell played a part but I think the main reason Anne Boleyn was charged with the most hideous crimes and then executed was this. You just plain hated her.

"By this time you could not stand the sight of her. You hated her very voice. She was bad-tempered and nagging. And to top all this she had not provided you with the male heir she had promised to. And of course you had fell in love with her lady-in-waiting Jane Seymour. Is any of this not true?"

Henry was stunned by the accusation but had to acknowledge that there was some truth in her words.

"I had come to dislike her, yes. But I would not have faked charges and executed her out of spite. I am a man of honour whatever you or your history books suggest."

"I think you would have done Henry. I believe you did just that. A man of honour! Don't make me laugh. You were, and probably still are, a spiteful man. And you had form. Thomas More was killed out of spite and Bishop Fisher. Wolsey would have been if he hadn't have died first. Four years after Anne's death Cromwell would be executed out of spite because he had arranged the doomed marriage to Anne of Cleves."

Henry felt his rage boiling over again.

"How dare you? Those men were executed after a trial. More and Fisher would not accept my break from Rome and preached against me. They were executed for treason not out of spite."

"They were accused of treason out of spite Henry. They defied you and stayed true to themselves and their God. They were brave men who knew, with a crazed despot like you as King, they were likely to die for doing so. But they did it anyway. It was they who were honourable men, not you. You killed them out of spite just like you killed Anne Boleyn. Cromwell helped, and advanced his own position, but he only took advantage of your hatred for Anne."

Henry felt the blood pounding in his ears.

"I DID NOT KILL ANNE. SHE WAS TRIED BY A COURT AND FOUND GUILTY."

"Yes you did Henry. You can scream and shout as much as you like but few believe you. Anne Boleyn and five innocent men died because you hated her. You killed them because you were an evil man. You killed them out of spite."

She walked back to the table, ignoring Henry who was beside himself with rage.

"Have you finished Miss Hussein?" asked the judge

"I have one further question for this witness My Lord."

"Go ahead,"

She turned to Henry who was seething.

"Henry, why was Mark Smeaton decapitated?"

Henry looked at her. He had once considered asking the same question.

"Because he was guilty."

"But he was a commoner. I can understand why the others were beheaded as they were of the nobility. But the normal sentence for a commoner found guilty of treason was death by being hung drawn and quartered. Is that not the case?"

"Broadly speaking, yes"

"So why was Mark Smeaton spared this gruesome fate?"

"I do not know?"

"And you never asked?"

"As I have said, I did not interfere with the judicial proceedings."

"I put it to you that the reason for this relative act of mercy was because he had co-operated with his interrogators by signing the confession."

"I do not know."

"But do you not think it is a possible reason?"

Henry looked at her for several seconds before replying.

"I suppose it is possible."

She turned to the judge.

"I have no further questions My Lord."

Chapter Thirteen

"How can she lie like that? Why is she allowed to?"
Lightfoot smiled.

"Are they lies? Was there not spite involved? Can you honestly say that?"

"So, even you, who are meant to defend me, believe her lies."

"Everyone believes it Henry. How could spite not be involved in some of your decisions? It is basic human nature. What we have to do is to convince the jury it wasn't the over-riding factor. We have to show them that, even though you detested Anne Boleyn, it was the charges against her and the fact she was found guilty by a court that ultimately decided her fate."

"But I saw the jury when that harridan was abusing me. They believed her."

"That was just her way of reimposing a commonly held belief about you. Henry, I am afraid you have been painted as one of the most spiteful men in history. The generally held view is that all the most high-profile executions stemmed from your personal pettiness and spite. People believe you killed pretty much anyone who displeased you."

"If they believe that what hope is there? This trial is just as much a foregone conclusion as the ones I am accused of orchestrating."

Lightfoot smiled.

"Relax Henry. Believe it or not I think today went pretty well-much better than I expected anyway."

Henry was flabbergasted.

"Are you insane? The jury believed her lies. I saw them nodding in agreement."

"You saw some agreeing and you saw just as many agreeing to the case we put. This is what a modern trial looks like. They accepted my case and then they accepted hers. In the end they will retire and work through that. But you did very well in there today Henry. I was surprised by how you largely kept your temper in check and how reasonable you seemed. And, if I was surprised and impressed so will the jury be."

"But she had the last word and surely that is crucial."

"It is important but when it comes to the final arguments I will have the final say. In truth, if the jury is diligent, and I see no reason why they won't be, it is not as crucial as you think."

Henry felt slightly reassured but the woman had angered him.

"She mocked me when I said I was an honourable man."

"To be fair Henry, honourable is the last word most would associate with you."

Henry was devastated. To him honour was everything, as it should be to all Kings. And for nearly 500 years his honour had been denied and his claim to it laughed at. For the first time he began to appreciate how history had judged him and he was mortified.

"It is unfair Lightfoot. It is very unfair."

"Is it Henry? Is it really? Even if you believed Anne and the others were guilty would an honourable man have so openly relished both the charge and the verdict? Would an honourable man not have ensured that they got at least a semblance of a fair trial? And would an honourable man have treated Catherine so badly? Would they have celebrated her death so? I could go on as there were plenty of other incidents when your behaviour appeared the very opposite of honourable."

Henry stared at him. No one had ever admonished him so and he was not given to self-criticism.

"If I behaved badly at times it was because there were other issues at play. Catherine's death meant England was safe from invasion and no one could any longer claim we were still married. And Anne's demise meant I was rid of her and free to marry Jane. I did relish it but I didn't bring it about."

"Well, I think we did make an impression with the jury on that last point. They now have to at least consider that you believed Anne was guilty. Given their pre-conceptions that is a major gain."

"But how can you make them believe she was guilty given how she has for so long been seen as a victim of false charges?"

"We don't have to. To be honest that is very unlikely to happen. The best we can do is to make them not so convinced that she was innocent. But Anne is not on trial here, you are. We don't have to convince them that Anne was guilty. We just have to make them consider that you believed she, and the others, probably were."

"And you think we did that?"

"Yes. Amira's cross-examination set us back a little but the new scenario of what happened is now in their minds. The fact you believed Anne was guilty will now be part of their discussions and that is the best we could have hoped for. And you also made a good impression on them. Again, Amira damaged that but she was on the back foot a little. Her last statements about you being spiteful sounded powerful but were really just a rehash of all historic depictions of you."

Henry was surprised.

"You think she was worried?"

"Probably not worried but she will now realise this is not going to be the cakewalk she thought it would be."

"So, you think we won today? It did not seem like that."

"Let us call it a losing draw. We are still on the backfoot. We may have made the jury re-consider a little where Anne Boleyn is concerned but there are plenty of other charges against you. And everything will be taken as a whole and that means Amira will keep coming up with examples of you being spiteful, evil and a down-right murderer."

Chapter Fourteen

The case against Henry the 8th in regard to Anne of Cleves

The Prosecution

"Your honour and members of the jury, this will be a little different. The prosecution has no specific charges against the defendant in this case. He has committed no crime that would deserve such a punishment that he rightly faces in the other cases. However, I think some examination is warranted as it will shed a light on his general behaviour, his selfishness and his lack of feeling for others. While these personal characteristics resulted in no vile crimes in this case they certainly did in others."

Amira Hussein turned to Henry.

"Henry, can we confirm several certain facts. Was it Cromwell who first mentioned the possibility of a marriage between you and Anne of Cleves?"

"Yes it was,"

"And his reason for this was to make an alliance with her brother William, who was a powerful Duke and a leader of the Protestant movement in what is now western Germany."

"That is correct."

"And this alliance was beneficial because your realm was under threat of attack from, among others, France and the Holy Roman Empire."

"Again you are correct."

"And is it true that you sent your court artist Holbein to paint a portrait of her?"

"Yes,"

"And did you, as legend has it, think her beautiful and then much less so when you saw her in the flesh."

"Yes. I had specifically asked Holbein not to exaggerate her beauty and I came to believe he did so. But it was not only him. There were many reports of her beauty and all were exaggerated. But it was not just her plain appearance. Her general demeanour was not attractive to me."

"I understand she was docile and obedient. After your strong opiniated first two wives I thought you would have relished that. Anne of Cleve's personality seems to have been like that of your third wife, Jane Seymour, who tragically died after giving you a son."

"There were similarities but Jane was educated and sophisticated while Anne was none of those things. Even her English was poor."

"I am intrigued why any of this would matter as it was a purely political marriage. You could still have your mistresses for your carnal desires."

"That is true but, and given your poor opinion of me this will surprise you, I wanted a loving marriage. I at least wanted a wife who could be a close confidant."

"Catherine of Aragon had been a close confidant and it didn't do her much good."

"She was and so was Jane in a different way. Anne Boleyn had been as well although she had proved to be a false friend. You have to understand that being a King can be very lonely. All my advisors had their own agendas. They all voiced an opinion that was likely to benefit them. A King has no real close friends. I could talk to Catherine and I knew I could trust her not to divulge my secrets to anyone. She also gave me sound advice."

"Ok, I accept that but surely you could have endured your dislike of Anne of Cleves for the benefits of the political alliance. All through history, and even in modern times, monarchs marry for largely political reasons."

"I didn't exactly dislike her. It was more that I found her unattractive in so many ways. But you are correct in that there was a far more important consideration. The fact was that even though Jane Seymour had provided me with a son the line of succession was still weak. My own elder brother had died before he could inherit the crown. The same could have happened to my son Edward."

"And of course we now know that Edward did die young. So, while you had an heir, you also needed a spare."

"I would not have expressed it so but yes."

"And then of course your lack of sexual attraction to Anne became a problem did it not?"

Henry felt his face redden even after all this time.

"Yes,"

"The marriage was never consummated, was it?"

"No it wasn't,"

"To put it bluntly you were unable to maintain an erection. You were rendered impotent."

The familiar feeling of shame washed over him again. He fought against it as he knew the embarrassment would lead to anger. It was what Lightfoot had warned him about. The Anne of Cleves marriage had not originally been part of the trial. Amira Hussein had only petitioned the judge to have it included after the conclusion of the Anne Boleyn case the day before. Lightfoot suspected it was because she was rattled but Henry knew why she had done it. She wanted to embarrass him and make him angry. Curiously Lightfoot had not opposed it.

"Yes, you are correct," he said as calmly as he could.

"And you blamed her for this?"

"She did not help matters. It was like she had never been taught what a wedding night entails."

"There were reports that you found her very odour repellent. Are they true?"

"Her perfumes were different to my previous women and I did not like it."

Amira Hussein smiled.

"At this stage in your life you were over-weight with pus coming out of your leg wound so I don't suppose it was much fun for her either."

Henry breathed deeply and just about managed to keep his temper in check.

"No, I suspect you are correct in that assumption."

She nodded slowly and Henry knew he had won at least a small victory by remaining calm.

"So, she had to go and, because of the political damage it would cause, you could not revert to your usual chop their heads off strategy."

"I finds your insults tiresome woman. Anne Boleyn was convicted by a jury. Anne of Cleves was never charged with any crime and so of course her life was never in danger from me."

"So, again the only option was annulment. Didn't this also become tiresome for you? You had at this stage had four marriages and three of them had been annulled. It was hardly a great example to your people was it? Didn't the new Anglican Church, of which you were head, not emphasise the sanctity of marriage?"

Again he managed to remain calm.

"There were special circumstances in my case."

"Really! I think most would say one rule for the peasants and a different one for the King. It is a case of do as I say not as I do. It is just selfish Henry. It is pure selfishness."

"You may claim that but a marriage not consummated is not a legal marriage. Practically every religion says that and I have been told that this is still true today."

"It is Henry. As I have said, you face no charges on this count. But I find it revealing and it undoubtedly had a massive bearing on what happened later. Who did you blame for the disastrous decision to marry Anne of Cleves?"

"I blamed Cromwell."

"Yes, your chief minister was to blame and not just for the marriage. To get an annulment you had to publicly state that the marriage had not been consummated. And this of course meant that you, the alpha male of all England, had been rendered impotent."

Henry glare at her and said coldly.

"Yes,"

She smiled.

"That must have been a touch embarrassing Henry. Even a man with your amazing lack of self-awareness must have known how this would greatly amuse your subjects. It must have created great mirth in every tavern in the country and, possibly worse, at court."

Henry gripped the rail in front of him. He remembered his rage as he thought about how the whole country had been laughing at him. Thousands of pamphlets had appeared mocking him as an impotent King.

"Again you are correct. I did know how it would amuse."

"And you blamed Cromwell for this public shaming and, as we will see later in the trial, this had major implications for him."

"Yes, I blamed Cromwell but he had committed no crime. It was nothing to do with his subsequent trial."

"Oh, you do make me laugh Henry. Do you really believe that your anger with him did not empower his enemies to move against him?"

Henry hesitated, knowing it was true.

"I concede that it may have had a bearing but I would remind you that I bestowed several more honours on him in the time between the Anne of Cleves affair and his trial."

She nodded.

"And I will concede that point. It is one that has baffled historians for years and one we shall examine later. But I personally believe it stems from your perverse and contradictory nature. But I have a further question. Why did you blame Cromwell at all?"

Henry was once again flabbergasted.

"Why would I not? He arranged the whole thing. He pushed for the marriage and I believe he pressurised Holbein to flatter Anne in the portrait. He signed the legally binding marriage contract which meant that if I backed out it would be an insult to those I hoped to make an alliance with. He was ultimately responsible for my need to explain why the marriage was not consummated."

"Yes, I accept all that and we now know that Cromwell was a much bigger supporter of the religious reformation cause than you imagined. It was almost certainly why he was so keen to align you with a protestant power in Europe. But Henry, you were the King. Cromwell gave you advice but you didn't have to take it. Why would anyone commit themselves to a marriage to someone they had never seen? Ultimately Henry, the only one to truly blame for the whole sorry debacle was yourself. Is that not true?"

"It was how things were done. You are right and I did blame myself but Cromwell failed me and a lot of the blame was his."

"Well, I see no record of you ever shouldering any blame publicly. Looking at your reign it suggests a pattern of behaviour. It is always someone else's fault. It was someone else's fault you married Catherine knowing she had been married to your brother. It was the Pope's fault for not going against centuries old church doctrine and granting you an annulment. It was Wolsey's fault for not convincing the Pope to change his mind. It was Anne Boleyn's fault because she bewitched you. It was Norfolk's fault that Cromwell was eventually executed. The only constant in your reign Henry is that you never took responsibility for your actions."

"A King has to rely on his councillors," he said stubbornly.

"And a real man has to accept responsibility."

Before he could answer she turned towards the judge.

"I have no further questions for this witness my Lord, on this case at least."

Chapter Fifteen

The case against Henry the 8th in regard to Anne of Cleves

The Defence

Lightfoot stood up slowly and walked to the centre of the room. This time he ignored the jury and looked at Henry.

"Henry, can I ask you a question that my esteemed colleague seems to have forgotten?"

"Of course,"

"What happened to Anne of Cleves after your marriage was annulled?"

"I gave her Richmond palace and Hever castle. I also settled an annual sum of money on her."

"Why did you treat her so generously?"

"Because she had not contested the annulment. The failed marriage was not her fault."

"Was the need to pacify her brother and family not also relevant?"

"Yes, but relations had improved, with France at least, and the alliance was no longer of such importance."

"But is it also true that you and her developed a close friendship? You wished her referred to as "The King's beloved sister". You made a decree that she would be given precedence over all women in England with the only exceptions being your wife and two daughters. For the rest of your reign she was treated very well. She was often invited to court. Is this all true?"

"Yes. I very much appreciated her easy acceptance of the annulment but later I came to enjoy her company. As her command of the English language got better, I found her personality much improved."

"And she went on to live her whole life in England in great comfort. Edward was close to her and she attended Mary's coronation. She eventually fell out of favour with Mary as she was close to Elizabeth but even then Mary did not move against her or strip her of her property."

"I understand this to be the case although of course I have only just been made aware of it."

Lighfoot turned and looked at the jury.

"You see Ladies and Gentlemen of the jury this is a side of Henry the 8th that you rarely see. It doesn't fit the narrative. It doesn't conform to the age old accepted view of him. No one is interested in a noble and honourable Henry as it makes things complicated. I am willing to bet very few of you knew how well treated Anne of Cleves was after her divorce. It is quite clear that my learned colleague for the prosecution has no desire to enlighten you on this particular piece of history. It would harm her case if she did so as it is so at odds with her view of Henry as a dishonourable, spiteful monster without feelings for others."

He walked towards the jury and again looked into the eyes of the lady he had seemingly picked out as a dominant figure.

"You see Ladies and Gentlemen of the Jury, the prosecution is correct. I am glad they decided to examine this case because, to use her words, it would shine a light on Henry's general behaviour. And it has done so. That light has shown us that Henry could be noble, fair-minded and honourable."

He walked alongside the jury bench and looked each of them in the eye before returning to the lady.

"And this behaviour came after he had faced what had to have been the most excruciating public humiliation. But, while he certainly held a grudge against his chief minister, he placed no blame on Anne of Cleves."

He looked at Henry before turning again to look at the woman in the front row of the jury.

"Now, I am sure council for the prosecution is going to say that he only behaved so well towards her because she meekly obeyed his commands. And she would be right. I don't think anyone can dispute that Henry was ruthless to those who crossed him and he was certainly often brutally unfair and even cruel. But it has to be remembered he was brought up to expect obedience from everyone. This was a man who believed he had been anointed by God. Everything has to be viewed in that context."

He walked back to his desk and stood by his chair.

"What this episode shows us is that Henry the 8th, contrary to popular belief, rewarded loyalty. It also demonstrates that he was often honourable, noble and even kind."

He looked at the judge.

"And on that note the defence rests on this particular case my Lord."

"Thank you Mr. Lightfoot. Miss Amira, you have the floor if you so choose."

She got to her feet and smiled.

"Thank you your honour but the council for the defence has kindly made the point I was about to. Ladies and Gentlemen of the jury, Henry was only kind to Anne of Cleves because she obeyed him. This is not a man who could abide anyone standing up to his bullying. He especially hated strong women as we saw in his behaviour towards Catherine and Anne Boleyn. In short, he was a very weak man who abused his position."

She again smiled at both the jury and the judge.

"And on that note the prosecution rests on this particular case my Lord."

Chapter Sixteen

The case against Henry the 8th in regard to Catherine Howard.

The Prosecution

Amira Hussein smiled at Henry before asking her first question. The woman fascinated him.

"How old was Catherine Howard when you married her Henry?"

"I believe she was seventeen."

"And how old were you?"

"I was forty-nine at the time."

She looked at the jury and smiled in a suggestive way. Henry noted that many smiled back at her.

"Even in your time would that age gap not normally have raised a few eyebrows?"

Henry was bemused.

"No, why would it?"

"Because you were probably older than her own father."

"It was not an issue."

"I know it wasn't because you, as King, could do pretty much as you liked. You saw a sexy young girl and you decided you wanted her and neither she or her family could object."

"Believe me, the Howards weren't going to object. It was what they had dreamed of. The Duke of Norfolk had once again got a niece of his to be my bride. And she raised no objection to being made a Queen, in fact she loved it."

"She had been made a Lady in waiting to Anne of Cleves. Is that right?"

"Yes,"

"And it was her uncle, the Duke of Norfolk, who arranged this position?"

"Yes,"

"And do you think he did this because he knew she might catch your eye?"

"Yes, he was always looking to strengthen his position."

"And it worked did it not? Norfolk, who had been marginalised since the Anne Boleyn affair, was now back at the top table."

"Norfolk had angered me over his role in the Anne Boleyn marriage but he remained a prominent member of my council. It wasn't just the new marriage to his niece that raised him in my estimation. He had served me well in a diplomatic mission to the French court."

"And of course this, on top of his role in the ill-fated marriage to Anne of Cleves, was a disaster for Thomas Cromell."

"Yes. It is well known that the two men were political rivals."

"Now, we are going to examine Cromwell's fall from favour later but is it not true that you married Catherine Howard on the very day he was executed."

"Yes, it is true."

"You see Henry, it is acts like this that show your true character. This man had served you so well. He had freed you, not just from the marriage to Catherine of Aragon, but from the Pope himself. When he first came to your court you were one of the poorest monarchs in the World. In four years he had made you one of the richest. Is all this correct?"

"It is true he served me well."

"But on the very day he died you married and celebrated wildly. I can imagine all the jokes you, Norfolk and the others had at his expense. How shameful. How horrible. How evil. It was like dancing on his grave-this man who had made you rich and powerful. Could you truly not spare a kind thought for him."

Henry gave this some consideration. Lightfoot had warned him that this was likely to be brought up.

"At the time I considered him a traitor. Later I came to consider that the charges against him were exaggerated and in some cases false. I regretted his death, and I regretted my actions that day. You are correct. It was poor behaviour."

"You regret your actions now, 450 years later, but there is no record of you doing so in your lifetime. And, as I have said before, it suggests a pattern of behaviour. You partied merrily when Catherine of Aragon died. You got engaged to Jane Seymour just one day after Anne Boleyn was executed. Let's face it Henry, you are a really vindictive, vengeful and petty person."

"It would not do for me to express regret at someone being executed for high treason. A King cannot be seen to be sympathetic to a convicted traitor. It would undermine the legal system and it could lead to the traitor being seen as a martyr to the public. This in turn could lead to rebellion."

"Your legal system needed undermining. It was a joke. The courts just did your bidding."

"I would refute that."

"Well, I will be providing ample examples of mine being the correct view. The truth is Henry, you were a dictator-a tyrant."

Henry looked at her and said calmy

"I would refute that."

"Tell me about your early impressions of Catherine Howard?"

"I found her exciting and joyous."

"Would you say you were captivated by her?"

"Yes,"

"And what did you end up thinking of her? What did you think of her as she was executed less than two years later?"

"I thought her a whore."

He heard a gasp from the jury but kept his eyes on Amira Hussein. She stared back at him for several seconds before replying.

"That judgement might seem harsh but history is kinder to you in this case Henry. Unlike the charges of adultery against Anne Boleyn, which most think false, the available evidence suggests that Catherine Howard might well have been guilty of the same charge. But there are aspects of your behaviour at the time that again seem suggestive of your true unpleasant nature."

"She was guilty of adultery on at least two counts. She spoke of my death to one of her lovers which is treason and, finally, she lied about her sexual history before our marriage. What was I meant to do? Was I to ignore it? Was I to take the ridicule of being a cuckold."

"Did she lie about her sexual history or did she just not divulge it? Was she even asked about it? I am sure seventeen-year-old girls of noble birth were expected to be virgins when they married."

"That is correct."

"So maybe no one asked her. Did You?"

"No, and you may be right in that no one asked her. But it makes no difference as she knew any sexual impropriety would make marriage to the King impossible."

"Was it a crime punishable by death to not divulge sexual history prior to marriage to the King?"

"Yes, as was inciting someone to commit adultery with her after the marriage."

"So, it would seem once again that everything was done according to the laws at the time."

"That is correct."

"Except it is not correct is it Henry? Catherine was stripped of the title of Queen and imprisoned on the 23rd of November 1541. Thomas Culpeper and Francis Dereham, her alleged lovers, were executed on the 10th of December 1541. Then on the 29th of January 1542 a bill passed through parliament that made it treason, and punishable by death, for a Queen to fail to disclose her sexual history or to incite someone to commit adultery with her. Is this not the same law you just referred to?"

"Yes,"

"So the law that she broke didn't actually exist when she broke it. Is that correct or am I missing something?"

"I believe the law allowed for retroactive implementation."

"You believe or you know?"

Henry sighed.

"I know,"

"Yes Henry, you know because you insisted upon it. Now does this seem fair to you? A person does something you don't like so you get parliament to make it a capital crime and then they are killed even though it wasn't a crime at the time. And you refute that you are a tyrant?"

"I could not force parliament to pass the law."

"No, but if they didn't you would just dismiss the parliament and appoint another that would obey your commands. Did you or did you not have this power?"

Henry felt his anger getting out of control.

"Yes, I had the power. A King must be the ultimate power in the land. Any parliament served in my name."

"So, parliament was, in reality, a sham."

"No, my realm had to have laws and those laws were passed by parliament, not me. I rarely interfered."

"But in this case, you did, didn't you? Did you or did you not make it known to your ministers in parliament that you wanted this law passed and you wanted it back-dated to ensure Catherine had broken it?"

Henry was seething now. For days he had held back and gone along with this circus. He had meekly accepted their insults and disrespect. But enough was enough.

"Yes, I did make it known. Lawyers argued that if she had had a pre-marriage contract with Dereham, and they had had sex, they would be legally married in the eyes of the church. That would make my marriage to her invalid and, in theory, she may not have committed a crime. I found the argument doubtful but also obscene. I refused to allow her to escape justice."

Amira Hussein smiled in triumph.

"So, your form of "Justice" was to condemn an eighteen-year-old girl to death?"

"He age was of no concern. Many girls of that age were routinely imprisoned or faced the death penalty for various crimes all over the country. At eighteen you know the difference between right and wrong."

"Oh, I am aware of the brutality of the legal system at that time. Children could be hung for stealing an apple. But it doesn't make it right Henry."

"But that is the way it was and for many centuries afterwards too. Who was I to change that? How can I be judged for just following the laws and conventions of the time?"

"You were the King, Henry. A good and noble King would have had some compassion for a young girl who had been used, abused and manipulated by older men all her life."

"Her crimes were not a one off. She tried to claim Dereham had forced himself on her but plenty of witnesses told of how she was a willing participant. She was not an innocent victim."

"Ok, let us examine that. Her mother died when she was four-years-old. She was put in the care of her father's step-mother, the Duchess of Norfolk, where, at twelve-years-old she came under the tutelage of one Henry Mannox. They began a relationship that both admitted was sexual in nature although both claim intercourse did not take place. Are all these details known to you?"

"I was made aware of it after later details of her depravity came to light."

"There is some dispute about the age of Mannox but it is clear that he was at least in his twenties while she was a child. We call that grooming Henry. We call it an abusive relationship between a man in a position of power and a child."

"The times were different but it is of no matter. The affair with Mannox was not one of the charges against her."

"It was not an affair Henry. It is what we now call rape as she was too young to give consent. Even if intercourse did not take place, and many suspect it did, he would now be jailed for several years for abusing his position as a teacher and an adult man. No blame would be attached to the child."

"But what relevance is that? The incidents did not take place in your time but mine."

"You are correct but it highlights that her first sexual encounters were at the hands of an older man-an older man who we can see was a sexual predator. For an impressionable child this might now seem normal. So when, a short time later, another older man, Dereham, made sexual overtures to her she responded as she had been conditioned to."

"It was still immoral and she would have known this."

"But can you not accept that the earlier relationship with Mannox had a bearing on the subsequent relationship with Dereham? She was used to being controlled by older men."

"No, I do not accept that."

"Oh, you are a hard man Henry. Can you at least accept that the second sexual relationship might not have taken place if the first hadn't."

"I see no reason to accept that either. It is a hypothetical question and I have no idea of the answer."

"Then you leave a void I suspect the jury will fill. She was used sexually by Mannox and then Dereham and then she was used politically by her family. I am sure the Duke of Norfolk had at least heard of the rumours about his niece's sexual history. But this didn't stop him putting her right in your line of sight when you wished to marry again. She was used Henry. She was used all her life including by you. You all used the poor girl and then you killed her."

"I didn't force her to marry me."

"Oh, come on Henry, do not treat us as fools. Girls of noble families did not have a choice in who they married. They were pawns in power games. What choice did she have? If she had refused to marry the King she would have been cast out by her family. She would have died in poverty."

"You cannot know that."

She smiled.

"No, you are right. I wasn't there. But you were Henry. You knew Norfolk. So, answer the question. Would he, as head of the family, have accepted her refusal to marry you easily? Would he have said that there was no problem Catherine, I just want you to be happy? Would he have said that Henry?"

Henry remembered Norfolk. He remembered him as a power-hungry bully who would have been as likely to say those words as he was to gouge his own eyes out. He nodded.

"I concede the point but she had ample time before the marriage to make her history known."

"And again, if she had done so, she would have been cast out by her family."

Henry hesitated.

"Again, I concede the point but you did not know her. If you did you would know that there was no way she was going to lose the chance to be Queen. She may, as you say, have been used but she was a willing participant."

"But, at just seventeen, did she know she was risking her life? Did she know the consequences of her actions? And did she know that, at some point, her history was bound to become known?"

"I cannot answer any of those questions other than to say she should have known."

"She was a child Henry. Can you imagine how exciting it was to be made Queen of England? Would any young girl not convince themselves that their secrets were safe?"

"She was not considered a child by the courts or even by society at the time."

"No, I would agree with that. In an age when many did not live past forty, seventeen is practically middle-aged. But that does not change the fact that she would have been naïve and inexperienced in the ways of the world. She made a massive mistake in not admitting her history but, considering the pressure she was under from her family, should she really have paid for that mistake with her life? Where is the compassion Henry?"

"A King cannot always show compassion. It could be seen as a sign of weakness and it could undermine the law."

"But you never even gave it any consideration did you? You went out of the way to make sure she was executed. Is that not true?"

"I wanted her punished, yes. I make no apologies for that. She had betrayed me with Dereham and also Culpeper who had been a favourite of mine. One could be seen as a mistake but two reveals her true character. She was a whore."

He saw her smile and he looked at Lightfoot who had his head in his hands. He had warned Henry about the use of the word and about insulting Catherine in general. But he was tired of apologising for his actions in life. He had done no wrong in this case. His wife, a mere girl, had cuckolded him, the King of England. How could she not expect death?

"I think you are wrong Henry. I think she was the victim of abuse in the case of Dereham and she was just a girl in love in the case of Thomas Culpeper."

"But she was not free to marry him. She was married to me, the King of England."

"But Culpeper met, and presumably fell in love with her, when she was a lady in waiting to Anne of Cleves."

"Does that excuse her infidelity? Does that excuse her betrayal of her husband and King? Should she, or he, not have mentioned this before my marriage to her?"

"No, it doesn't excuse her. None of what you say is wrong but it was not as simple as that was it? When you proposed marriage to her, or to anyone, it was an order in all but name."

"No, I do not accept that. She could have refused. I would have been unhappy, and I would have banished her from court, but I would not have forced the issue."

"But her family, and Norfolk in particular, would have. She had no real choice in the matter."

"As I have said before, she was far from unhappy at my proposal."

"And as I have said before, you can understand that. What young girl would not have wanted to be a Queen? But she was too young to know the implications of it. She was a young girl married to an over-weight, late middle-aged man with serious health problems. And every day she saw the young virile man she genuinely loved. Can you have no sympathy with her situation?"

Henry banged on the rail in frustration.

"Sympathy! Are you mad woman? It was adultery, plain and simple? She wanted the prestige of being my Queen and the carnal excitement and pleasure of her young lover. This is not some romantic love story. It is a squalid and sordid affair and an affront to God."

She smiled.

"And here we once again have to mention the many mistresses you had during all your marriages. You love your double standards don't you Henry."

"I was King and every King has mistresses. I did not hide it or them. There was no betrayal involved. It may be at odds with your modern morals and it may offend you. But that is how it was and, to a certain extent, still is."

"I would concede that point Henry but, even allowing for the different times and morals, how is her having sex with a man outside of her marriage an affront to God and you having sex with a woman outside of marriage not?"

Henry thought about his answer for some time and then nodded.

"I see your point but it is not the same. As I said, there was no betrayal involved. I was true in my heart to all my wives. My mistresses never had the same status. My wife was always first lady at court and in the country. I discovered that I was not first in Catherine Howard's heart. That honour belonged to Culpeper. And that was true betrayal."

Henry was pleased to hear a murmur of agreement from the jury. Lightfoot was also looking slightly happier. Seeming to catch the mood of the court Amira Hussein nodded in agreement.

"You make a good point Henry. I still feel your morals are twisted, and that you practice double standards, but I do concede that an emotional betrayal is worse than a purely physical one. But, even though I sympathise with your hurt feelings, and recognise the anger you would have rightfully felt, I can't help feeling your revenge was too terrible and out of proportion to the crime."

"It was treason. It was treason with both Dereham and Culpeper."

"No Henry, it was abuse of a child by Dereham and love with Culpeper."

"Dereham was heard to say he would take my place in her bed and heart if I was to die. To speak of the Kings death is to wish the Kings death. That was the law. That was treason. It was not true in Dereham's case, but it was in Culpeper's. Both men wished me dead and if they were guilty so was she."

"There is no historical evidence that Culpeper ever said these words or words like them."

"Not these words but a letter from Catherine was found in his rooms that made clear their feelings for each other. Do you really think young lovers do not talk of the death of the older husband who is a barrier to their happiness?"

"Yes, I am sure they do but that does not mean they are planning his death."

"Do you not understand woman? Adultery was not a capital crime in the general populace but adultery with the Queen was. If they had had a child they would have passed it off as mine and a false King may have come to the throne. That is treason. How could anyone deny that?"

Again, there was a murmur of agreement. Amira Hussein nodded.

"Yes, you are right on this point. No one can deny it but are you sure sexual intercourse even took place. The letter is full of love but no reference is made to sex. Historians are split on this but a small majority think that there was no intercourse. From reading the letter myself that would also be my conclusion."

"Lady Rochford, Catherine's senior lady in waiting, confessed that she had stood guard outside the Queens rooms while she entertained Culpeper. She also helped him escape unseen. This, together with the letter, makes a very convincing case that their relationship was a sexual one. I think only a fool who could not face the truth would think otherwise."

"But was not Lady Rochford threatened with torture before admitting this?"

"I know not and I care not. But I have no doubt her evidence was the truth."

"A person facing torture may say whatever the interrogator asks. I understand this was Archbishop Cranmer. He was a political and religious rival of the

Duke of Norfolk. Would he not have wanted to bring the family down?"

"So, now Cromwell is dead you are blaming everything on Cranmer. Lady Rochford knew she faced execution herself. Faced with her own death she would not have lied under oath. Unlike your modern times people were protective of their mortal soul. Can you not accept that, in this case at least, the evidence supports the official version. Catherine and her lovers were guilty."

Amira Hussein smiled.

"You make a good point about it being a fearful thing to lie under oath and it is one I will be returning to. The same could be said of Anne Boleyn and her alleged lovers who all denied the charges after swearing on the bible. But in this case your point is valid. Catherine Howard was probably guilty of treason under the laws of the time. The question is could you not have been lenient to a young foolish girl. Why did you have to snuff out her life?"

Henry looked at her in exasperation.

"She committed treason and there is only one penalty for treason. Even if I had wanted to be lenient, which I didn't, I would have been a fool to do so. My throne was not safe. I was only the second Tudor King and the supporters of the house of York still questioned my right to be King. Treason had to be punishable by death or I would be other-thrown as I would have been seen as weak."

"No, I don't buy that. I think you would have been seen as just and fair. Everyone must have known that Catherine was just a pawn in the power games of her family. Your popularity would have gone up in the country but instead you came to be seen as a brutal, vengeful tyrant who murdered a young stupid girl."

"A King cannot allow concerns of popularity to stop him from doing what must be done."

"Oh, come on Henry, It didn't have to be done. Let's face it, you made sure she was executed because you were angry at being cuckolded and humiliated by a teenage girl. Banishment from court for her and close members of her family would have sufficed."

"I followed the law and protected my throne."

"No you didn't Henry. Only a fool would believe sparing her life would endanger your throne. Everyone in the country knew she was a pawn who had had no choice but to marry you. Everyone then, and throughout history, knew she had been used by powerful men all her life. And you knew it too Henry. You knew it but you didn't care. All you were concerned with was that she had embarrassed you and for that she had to die.

"And so you killed her Henry. You destroyed a life. She had been used and abused all her life and then it was her misfortune to meet one of the most evil men in history. And for him it was never going to be enough to use and abuse her. You were much worse than all the others Henry. You were worse than Mannox, Dereham and her uncle, Norfolk. You were worse because, when you were finished using her, you chopped the poor girls head off."

Henry glared at her-his eyes full of rage.

"I did not use her. I married her and made her Queen of England. She committed treason and was executed according to the law after a fair trial."

Amira Hussein smiled.

"And Lady Rochford, who we spoke about earlier, was she executed after a fair trial?"

Henry glared at her.

"She facilitated the betrayal. She allowed Culpeper into my wife's room and stood guard outside while they fornicated. She was guilty of treason."

"That wasn't the question, Henry. Was she executed after a fair trial?"

"As I am sure you know she was condemned by an act of attainder."

"Oh yes, of course. Your obedient parliament passed a bill condemning her to death. This was because she had had a complete mental breakdown and under the law she was not medically fit to stand trial. But again, you weren't going to allow a little thing like the law to stand in the way of your vengeance. How can you still claim to respect the law. It would be laughable if so many people hadn't have been killed. You murdered a woman who had lost her mind. Because your pride was hurt you murdered an imbecile. You are a monster Henry. You are evil personified."

"She was faking it. She was clever and manipulative. She was older and supposedly wiser than Catherine. It was part of her job as lady in waiting to steer Catherine in the right direction. But instead she encouraged her to become a whore and to betray me. I think it was her idea of revenge for the death of her husband."

"Oh yes, her husband George Boleyn, who we are supposed to believe committed incest with his sister Anne."

"I believe it."

"Maybe you really do Henry but I suspect you have made yourself believe it. You won't find many people who share that belief. But back to Lady Rochford. Did you not ride roughshod over the law to have her executed?"

Henry glared at her for several seconds before replying in a defiant voice.

"No, what I did was stop her from using the law to her advantage. She was a traitor and I was determined that she would die a traitors death."

Amira Hussein turned to the judge.

"That concludes the prosecution's case in regard to Catherine Howard My Lord."

Chapter Seventeen

The case against Henry the 8th in regard to Catherine Howard

The Defence

"Ladies and Gentlemen of the jury, I shall not dwell long on this case as my client has already defended himself admirably. I am surprised my learned friend spent so much time on it as, in law, there is no real charge. And when I say law I don't just mean the law in the 16th Century. It is the same now. In this case there is little doubt, even among historians. Most agree that Catherine was guilty of treason and the punishment for treason was death."

Lightfoot turned to look at Henry.

"Now, of course Henry could have used his position to commute the sentence but, as he has said, there were dangers involved with that. What we now call the war of the roses had raged for over thirty-two years. It is thought that over 105,000 people died which is a low estimate. During that time several men came to rule England and what they all come to learn was that any sign of weakness could, and in some cases did, cost them the throne and their lives."

He looked at the jury and back again to Henry before continuing.

"At times it was unbelievably brutal. Monarchs and feudal barons murdered close members of their own families. Richard the Third probably killed his two young nephews because they had a much stronger claim to the throne than him. If he didn't kill them my client's father, Henry the 7th almost certainly did. And it is in this context that we have to see Henry's decision not to spare Catherine's life. He could never show weakness where treason was concerned."

"Henry, how many rebellions were there during your reign?"

"There were many-often two a year. Some were put down easily but at least six were major threats."

"And these were mainly about your changes to the Church?"

"Yes, but there were also claims of corruption and general dissatisfaction. There were also still a few false claimants to my throne."

Lightfoot turned towards the jury.

"So, you can see how it was. The middle-ages were a brutal time and for a King to survive he had to be extra brutal. Leniency could be fatal. And if you don't believe me consider another seventeen-year-old.

"Lady Jane Grey was named as successor to the throne by Henry's son Edward to stop the Catholic Mary from inheriting the throne. The people rebelled and Mary became Queen. She was well aware that Jane had been used as a pawn by her ambitious family and so, even though she had been found guilty of treason, Mary spared her life. The consequence of that leniency was another plot to remove Mary and once again put Jane on the throne. So this time she was executed.

"It wasn't fair or just but while she was alive usurpers would always rally round her and declare her the true Queen. So the threat had to be removed. Mary was to make the same mistake later when supporters of the new protestant religion promoted the claims of her sister Elizabeth. But Elizabeth did learn the lesson well. She, like her father, was not soft on treason and hers was a long and successful reign."

He looked again at the single female juror.

"Now, you might argue that all this is not relevant in this case. Catherine Howard was not involved in a plot to dethrone Henry. She was not a threat to his reign like Jane Grey would be to Mary. But you would be wrong. If Catherine had a child with Culpeper and passed it off as Henry's it is the end of the Tudor line. If it was discovered, or even suspected, it could have led to as brutal a conflict as the war of the roses itself. Make no mistake, it was the highest form of treason."

He turned from the jury and walked towards Henry.

"But, while we can see why you felt you could show no leniency there is one question my learned friend brought up that I would like to examine. Why did you insist on a law change that retroactively covered Catherine's betrayal of you? That does seem vindictive and unfair."

"Because, if I had not she might well have escaped the axe. I do not deny I felt a personal enmity to her but it was as you explained before. If she did not die she would have been perceived to have not paid the ultimate price for treason. I would have been seen as weak."

"So, let us be clear. If she could prove that her and Dereham had made a pre-contract of marriage and then they had had sex they would have been married in the eyes of the Church?"

"Yes,"

"And that would mean she had never been legally married to you?"

"That is correct."

"And that would mean she could not have committed adultery, against you at least, as she had never been married to you?"

"That is what my ministers told me."

"But when she was first interrogated, and this was first put to her, she denied that there was a pre-marriage contract or that she had had sex with Dereham?"

"Yes, but she could have backtracked on this at any point. I wanted the law so it would cover any future wife and I did not think it needed to be backtracked. To me Catherine was plainly guilty but Cranmer advised me to cover any eventuality."

"Was there also an element of making an example of her-a sort of statement to say, this is what happens when you humiliate a King?"

Henry looked at him steadily.

"Yes, I would not deny that. I would be foolish not to send out a message like that. My throne and life would be at risk if I allowed crimes against me to go unpunished."

Lightfoot turned to face the jury.

"So, there we have it ladies and gentlemen of the jury. Henry Tudor was a King and Kings often have to be ruthless. Sometimes leniency and mercy can be very dangerous. This was especially true in Henry's time. He had powerful enemies everywhere, not least the entire Roman Catholic religion. As King of England Henry felt he had no choice. Catherine Howard had committed treason and she had to pay the ultimate price for that treason.

"But Henry Tudor was also a man. He was a human being and, as such, he had human faults. He could be jealous, angry and selfish. He could also, when betrayed and humiliated, be cruel, vindictive and, given his position, deadly. But is he so different to any man. How many men who are publicly cuckolded are magnanimous? I know I wouldn't be.

"Now, it may be argued that very few other men would have made sure the people who had humiliated him were killed. But Henry was also King. He wasn't just humiliated. Catherine Howard and her lovers had, in his eyes at least, endangered the whole Tudor line. They may even have plotted his own death.

"Some of you, quite naturally, might consider that this threat was over-blown and that he could have shown some leniency towards a young girl. That is arguable. It is impossible not to have sympathy for Catherine. She had been used, and almost certainly sexually abused, all her life. She never really had any choice when Henry proposed. She would have been cast out by her family if she refused and, given her privileged background, this would have been a virtual death sentence.

"But, despite our sympathy, we must accept that Catherine Howard was not murdered. It is a tragic story, and Henry did not behave well, but she was almost certainly guilty of a crime that carried the death penalty."

Henry walked along the jury bench and looked each juror in the eye while he continued.

"Now, some of you may still think Henry was too ruthless but consider this. If this was the only charge against Henry would he be here facing the ultimate penalty? Would he be facing the prospect of his soul burning in hell for all eternity? I will assure you he wouldn't, because, in this case at least, he stayed within the boundaries of the law at the time. Unlike the Anne Boleyn case there is little evidence of trumped up charges.

"No ladies and gentlemen of the jury, in regard to Catherine Howard, Henry has no case to answer."

He turned to the judge.

"That concludes the defence in regard to Catherine Howard My Lord."

"Miss Hussein, do you wish to cross-examine this witness?"

"I have a couple of questions My Lord."

"Go ahead."

She turned to Henry.

"Henry, would you agree that in your time daughters of high-born families were not free to marry who they liked?"

"Yes, I would agree."

"Would you also agree that they had very little freedom of choice in any aspect of their lives?"

"Daughters obeyed their father's, yes. I will never see that as wrong. Is it so different now."

"No, not in a lot of countries anyway. But my point is this. When you asked her to marry you, she would have had no choice. Her father and uncle would have insisted on it. Do you not agree."

"She should have told me, and them, why a marriage between us was impossible."

"Did you never consider that her father and uncle must have known. Her relationships with Dereham were an open secret in the house in which she grew up in. A lot of the servants gave evidence to that effect. So are we really to believe that her father wouldn't have known. I suspect he would have made it his business to know of any potential threat to the marriage. From all I have read of Norfolk I am sure he would have too."

"You are right. His stepmother, the Dowager Duchess of Norfolk certainly knew."

"But they made no mention of it to you. Norfolk was one of the highest men in the land and one of your closest advisors but he did not set the record straight. He did not whisper in your ear that the marriage may not be wise."

"No, but I can't say for sure that he knew."

"If you were sure that he knew do you think it would have made a difference? Would he have told you the truth about his niece?"

"No, certainly not. He was a very ambitious man and he would see how having his niece as Queen would benefit him and his family."

"So, I think we can also assume that he would be livid if Catherine had refused to marry you."

"He would have been very angry, yes."

"And with good reason too as I am sure you would have seen any refusal as an insult. And the family, and Norfolk in particular, would have suffered consequences. They would be very much out of favour with you and we have seen how dangerous that can be."

"It is true that I would have been unhappy with Norfolk and her father."

"And you would be angry with them rather than Catherine. Is that not so?"

"Yes as I would expect them to have more control over their daughter."

"As you had over your daughters, nieces and sisters. All would have had to marry who you chose. Is that not so?"

"Of course. That is how treaties and alliances are made."

"And how is that different to Norfolk, as head of his family, not insisting his niece marry you."

"It is not different. It was how things were done in the nobility."

"So, Catherine has no choice but to marry you but it is her rather than the male head of the family who suffers the consequences when it goes wrong. Can you not see how grossly unfair that is?"

Henry hesitated realising he had been led into a trap.

"Norfolk did fall out of favour, and the Dowager Duchess was sent to the tower but, in the end, it was Catherine's crime not his."

"So his niece died and his step-mother was imprisoned. And if Norfolk fell out of favour it was for mere days as he didn't lose his place on the council and he seemed as powerful as ever. You really didn't like women much did you Henry?"

Henry felt his face redden as the jury laughed.

"Is that not true Henry? It was always the women who suffered under your rule. Catherine of Aragon was divorced and imprisoned for life while you happily remarried and lived life to the full. Anne Boleyn died but her father kept all his lands. And now young Catherine has her head chopped off while her uncle, who had at the least encouraged the marriage, kept all his lands, titles and power. You are a misogynist Henry. It is as simple as that."

Before he could reply she turned to the Jury.

"Ladies and Gentlemen of the jury, the defence is trying to claim that Catherine Howard was killed because Henry dare not show leniency where treason is concerned. They claim that his personal anger, humiliation and vindictiveness was secondary. I do not buy it. In fact I consider it poppy-cock.

"All through his life his personal feelings were the driving force. Sparing Catherine's life was never going to cause rebellion in the country. And it might be argued that why should her lovers be killed why she is spared? I will tell you why. Her lover were adults who had a choice. Dereham took sexual advantage of a vulnerable child and later blackmailed her so he could gain high office at court. Culpeper was a personal favourite of the King.

"Both of them could choose their actions. But Catherine Howard had rarely got to choose anything in her short life. She was forced into a relationship with Dereham, and she was forced into marriage with Henry. The king should have recognised this and spared her. He could have banished her from court and sent her, in disgrace, back to her family home.

"Even if she wasn't cast out she would never have been seen again. Her family would have seen to that. In that time social death was almost as bad as the real thing.

"But Henry couldn't do that. He had to have his pound of flesh. It was little to do with the danger in showing leniency for treason. It was revenge, pure and simple. I find it obscene that her vile uncle, the Duke of Norfolk, survived and prospered while she died.

"But Norfolk was a powerful man. He commanded armies that were loyal to Henry. He was a man useful to Henry while his niece was a worthless female and, as such, she could be killed without a second thought."

She turned to the judge.

"That concludes my cross-examination in this case My Lord."

Chapter Eighteen

"Why does she hate me so?"

Lightfoot gave him a half-smile.

"I wouldn't take it personally. It is her job to make you out to be an evil murderer."

"No, I think she really believes it. I can see it in her eyes."

"You may be right. The trouble is Henry she is a woman, and you don't have a great reputation for treating women well."

Henry walked to the window. Outside he could see the deer grazing in the sun. He felt unexpectedly hurt by Lightfoot's accusation.

"It is unfair. I treated women with respect and kindness. The deaths of Anne Boleyn and Catherine Howard give a false impression."

"And your treatment of Catherine of Aragon, your daughters and sisters? There were several other women who were executed after you had pushed for such a sentence."

"I treated my daughters well."

"Really? Mary was denied access to her mother and was not even allowed to visit her on her deathbed. Both daughters were pronounced as bastards at some point."

"It was different times. There were good reasons why I acted as I did."

Lightfoot sighed.

"There may well have been but Amira believes you are a woman-hater and she has possibly got a majority of the jury agreeing with her."

Henry walked back to his seat. He felt tired and sad.

"It was not meant to be this way Lightfoot. I wanted to be a just King. It started so well. I truly loved Catherine and she helped me greatly in the early years. If God could have blessed us with a male child I would have loved and cared for her all my days.

"There would have been no need to break with Rome. Anne Boleyn and Catherine Howard would have lived as would Norris and the others. How did it go so wrong? I did not want to be a tyrant like the usurper Richard of York and so many others. I wanted to be loyal and fair to my subjects. I wanted to build a new England. How did I end up hated by history?"

"Many years after your death a wise man noted that power corrupts, and absolute power corrupts absolutely."

Henry considered this then nodded.

"Yes, that sounds right. I was bitter and angry later in my life. I thought I was at odds with God."

"You were also in a lot of pain weren't you?"

"Yes, I had a leg wound that wouldn't heal. I grew fat as I could not exercise or take part in tournaments. I have never told anyone but I felt half a man. With the exception of Anne of Cleves I always married for love Lightfoot. I never considered politics like Kings are supposed to."

"This would reflect well on you if you hadn't executed two of them and treated another quite abominably."

"Do you think I should have let Catherine Howard live?"

"Yes but, and I want you to be honest, do you think that in the earlier days of your reign you would have been so determined to see her executed? You said you wanted to be a just and fair King. And if this is true would you not have considered her age and the fact she had been used by Dereham, Culpeper and her uncle?"

Henry thought about it for a considerable time.

"I do not know. I would like to think so. I think I was more open to clemency then. But I can't honestly say I would have. Catherine was not the innocent that you and that woman make out. I accept she was ill-used by men but she also ill-used me. Did that woman harm my case?"

"Her name is Amira. Yes, she played it very well. We, and you especially, had done very well. The jury has seen a different view on Catherine's execution and that will still be in their minds. But casting you as a misogynist was a smart move. With the available evidence it is hard to argue against it. Half the jurors are women and all the men have lived in an era where women have equal rights."

"I find that so strange. Women should obey their husbands. Do they not have to swear it in their wedding vows?"

Lightfoot smiled.

"Not any more Henry, not anymore."

Chapter Nineteen

The case against Henry the 8th in regard to Catherine Parr.

The Prosecution

"What was it that attracted you to Catherine Parr, Henry?"

Henry looked at Amira Hussein. It was an innocuous question but he now knew that there was a purpose behind everything she said.

"I found her intelligent, lively, and strong. I also thought her good-natured and attractive."

"Would it be fair to say that you had a lot more in common with her than you did with your second, third, fourth and fifth wives?"

"Yes, that would be fair."

"You found her good company and a calming influence?"

"Yes,"

"You were good friends?"

"Yes,"

"You held her in such high regard that you appointed her regent when you were away fighting in France. You, in effect, left your realm in her hands?"

"Yes, I did."

"Were you aware that, before you married her, she had started a romance with Thomas Seymour, the brother of your third wife, Jane?"

"I was aware they were on friendly terms but I did not know it was a romantic friendship. I was assured no promises had been made."

"So it was a coincidence that he was given a diplomatic posting in Brussels at about the same time?"

"His name was put forward, as many were, and I approved the posting. It was a very prestigious position at that."

"I am sure it was but are we truly to believe that the fond feelings between him and your new wife did not play a part in your decision to appoint him to a role far from court?"

Henry paused before replying.

"No, you are correct. I will admit that. Although he was worthy of the role, his closeness to Catherine was a factor. Although I did not doubt their loyalty to me I thought it best for all concerned if there was space between them."

Amira Hussein turned towards Lightfoot and smiled before turning back to Henry.

"I see my learned friend has coached you well Henry. Again you act in complete contrast to your reputation. You admit mistakes and appear honest, sensible and reasonable. But it must be hard Henry and I wonder how long you can keep the pretence up. I do not think it will be long before your true nature rears its ugly head."

"Have you never considered that this is my true nature and that my reputation, that is based on the views of historians and story-tellers who were born centuries after my death, is false?"

"Yes, I have considered that Henry. I have given it due consideration and I have dismissed the idea. I did so because the hard facts, as well as historical letters and records, do not support it. What they suggest is that you cannot fail to have known that they were romantically involved. It was an open secret and there are surviving letters to support that view."

"As I said, no promises had been made. If they had been Catherine would not have married me and I would not have asked her to."

"Oh, come on Henry, you knew a proposal from you was pretty much a command. She was not ordered to by a father, or a bully of an uncle, as Catherine Howard had been, but her family would have suffered a fall from grace if she had refused. She is on record as saying it was her duty to marry you."

"None of that is true."

"Oh, I think it is Henry. I, and pretty much everyone who has studied you, know that your anger and spitefulness would have known no bounds if she had refused."

"Catherine Parr was a strong person. If she did not want to marry me, she would not have done so. She married me because she wanted to."

"Is that true Henry? By that time your reputation as a wife killer was known across Europe. On being told she was being considered as your bride did not Princess Christina of Denmark say "If I had two heads, I would happily put one at the disposal of the king of England" Did you not hear of this?"

Henry felt his cheeks colour. He remembered his rage when he discovered the remark had been common knowledge long before anyone had been brave enough to tell him. He had been a laughing stock across all Europe.

"Yes, I heard of it,"

"So would a sensible woman like Catherine Parr want to marry you knowing that two previous wives had ended up headless?"

"I say again that Anne Boleyn and Catherine of Howard were guilty of treason. If Catherine Parr was a good and loyal wife, she had no need to fear me. And she clearly didn't as she accepted my proposal."

"Would you have accepted her refusal with good grace?"

Henry hesitated. In truth he had never even considered that she might refuse.

"I would have been angry but I would have had no choice but to accept it."

"So Catherine and her family would not have suffered any loss of social standing at court. They would not have been passed over for high office. Is this true Henry because the historical records suggest otherwise? They show, especially later in your reign, that anyone denying you anything was finished at court. This also included their families.

"We all know what happened to Catherine of Aragon when she denied you and she was the lucky one. Wolsey, More and Cromwell were all accused of treason and this is how you saw it isn't it Henry? This is the basis of your entire life. It was nothing to do with evidence and trials. It was simply that you believed that anyone who denied you what you wanted was guilty of treason. And that is how you would have seen Catherine Parr's refusal. Is that not so?"

"No, it is not."

"Yes it is Henry. You believed you were chosen by God to be King so it follows that anyone who goes against you goes against God himself."

"No, that is a false interpretation of my position."

"How is it false? Did you not believe you, and your father before you, were Kings by God's hand?"

"Yes, I believed that and still do."

"So how is my argument wrong? How could anyone denying you not also be denying God?"

Henry felt flustered and confused. He looked at Lightfoot in desperation and to his relief he stood up.

"I object My Lord. The council for the prosecution is falsifying a monarch's position. Any King of that time, and any other time, would believe they were appointed by God. It didn't mean that they could not be contradicted or denied. That would mean they actually saw themselves as God."

"Miss Hussein," said the judge.

"I think, that for some Kings, it could well mean they could not be contradicted or denied. And I also believe that some could even come to see themselves as God. And I believe the jury should be allowed to consider if Henry was such a King as there is ample evidence that he was."

The judge nodded.

"I agree and I will allow you to continue with this line of questioning."

Amira Hussein turned towards Henry.

"So Henry, please answer the question. If you believed you were appointed by God how could anyone denying you not also be denying God?"

Henry paused but Lightfoot's objection, even though it was not granted, had bought him some time.

"Even though I believe I was appointed by God I was aware of my own humanity and of my own human failings. I knew I could err, and even sin, and would need wise council at times. I did not believe I was God and that is a foul insult."

"Catherine of Aragon, Thomas Wolsey, Thomas More and Thomas Cromwell all gave you wise council at times but you ended up turning on them all. It seems you only wanted their council when it suited your agenda. When it didn't you accused the latter three of treason. Is that not the behaviour of a man who has come to believe in his divine right?"

"The three you mention all had their own agenda's which were in opposition to mine. I regretted the need to charge them as they had served me well but they were guilty of treason. I acted as a King, not a God."

"So, do you believe most Kings would have done the same?"

"Of course, and many did. Do you think Philip of Spain or Charles the 5th did not execute councillors who worked against them?"

"Ok, I accept your point but how many Kings do you know who changed the whole religion of their country?"

Henry heard a murmur of agreement from the jury.

"I did not change the religion. I just made myself head of it in my country."

She laughed.

"Oh, is that all? Do you think that is a small thing? You changed a religion that had been followed in England for over a thousand years. And you did so just because you wanted to marry again. I would say that is the act of a man who has come to believe that he is God."

"You have no idea of how it hurts me when you say such a thing. I love God and I would rather die than to consider myself his equal."

"Your outrage is meaningless. It doesn't make it any less true. But I will leave it to the jury to decide if your actions support my view. But now let us return to your last marriage. You have stated that Catherine Parr was free to refuse you with no consequences for her or her family. Do you stand by that?"

"Yes, I do,"

"You have also stated that, despite your awful record in disposing of your wives, she had nothing to fear from you if she was a good and loyal wife. Is that true?"

"Yes, it is."

"And yet, less than three years into the marriage, a warrant for her arrest was drawn up on your command. The charge was heresy and if found guilty, and let's face it, they were always found guilty, she would have been burnt at the stake or beheaded. So it seems she did have something to fear from marrying you."

Henry heard at least one member of the audience gasp.

"That was a mistake that was quickly rectified."

"How was it a mistake? Bishop Stephen Gardiner overheard a conversation between you and Catherine about the protestant cause, which she supported. After she departed, he told you her views were heretical. You agreed and when he drew up the arrest warrant you signed it. Where was the mistake?"

"Gardiner misunderstood her words. She only discussed religion with me to learn and to understand."

"So, did you also misunderstand as well?"

"Yes. I was not in good health at the time and my judgement was flawed."

"She came to you did she not and made it clear what she meant? She also begged you not to misunderstand and that she would aways refer herself to your better judgement. You then declared that all misunderstandings were over and that you were friends again. And when the men came to arrest her, you dismissed them and rescinded the warrant. Is that broadly how it was?"

"Yes,"

"Yes, and that is all very sweet but I wonder what would have happened if a brave person had not leaked news of the imminent arrest to her. If she had not had the chance to explain it to you she would have been arrested, imprisoned and almost certainly executed. It was pure chance that she survived. Is that not the case?"

"No, she would have had the chance to explain her words."

"Would she really Henry? Your record does not support this. After Anne Boleyn was arrested, she never saw you again. It was the same with Henry Norris, Francis Weston and William Brereton. Catherine Howard was denied an audience with you as was Thomas Cromwell. It would seem that when they were arrested that was pretty much it. An arrest warrant was in reality a death warrant. Why would it have been different for Catherine Parr?"

"They all had a chance to explain themselves at their trials."

"And they all did. George Boleyn is supposed to have made such a brilliant defence that most thought he would be acquitted. But it did him and the rest no good at all. The court by this stage took an arrest warrant signed by you as a directive to find them guilty. I am sure you will deny that but the sheer amount of victims make your protests laughable."

"I do not accept that. People were found not guilty in my courts."

"I am sure some were but not when it was made clear that was not the verdict you wanted."

"I would not have wished Catherine Parr's death."

"I suspect you wouldn't but would you have had the moral courage to stand up to Bishop Gardiner? The conservatives, such as Gardiner, were in the ascendancy as you were concerned with the rise of the protestant movement. If Catherine was publicly accused of heresy would you have allowed her to be acquitted?"

"It would not have been my choice. It would have been a matter for the judges."

"The judges you had ultimately appointed?"

"They were honourable men."

"They were scared men Henry. By 1546 everyone in high office was scared as one wrong move and they were dead. They were either in favour with you or in the tower awaiting execution. That was the reality of your court. Your moods and religious views changed constantly. One moment the reformers such as Cromwell had your support and then the conservatives like Gardiner did.

"In that climate of fear no one was going to go against your wishes. If Catherine was put on trial the judges would have assumed you wanted her gone. It would have been viewed the same as in the Anne Boleyn case."

"The cases were not the same. The arrest warrant for Catherine Parr was just a misunderstanding. I don't believe there would ever have been a trial and certainly not an execution."

Amira Hussein smiled.

"That is easy to say now but it is hard to see how she would ever have had a chance to clear up that misunderstanding, given your track record, if she had not received prior warning. But we will leave that to the jury to decide.

"What I would ask is why you were so easily swayed by Bishop Gardiner? For two years you had been happily married and you had even appointed Catherine regent for a time. And yet Gardiner, who seems a sneaky bastard by the way, eavesdrops on a private conversation and you immediately comply when he accuses Catherine of heresy. Why did you do that Henry? Were you really that weak?"

"I was never weak," roared Henry. "How dare you accuse me of weakness?"

"I dare because it seems weak. In fact, it appears pitiful. A proper man would have had Gardiner arrested for eavesdropping on his King."

"It was not weakness. Catherine had angered me with her views and Gardiner took advantage of this anger. He was a staunch conservative and suspected, possibly correctly, that Catherine was trying to turn me to the protestant cause. I regretted my reaction to his words almost instantly and at the first opportunity I rescinded the arrest warrant."

"That is maybe true, although I still suspect she would have ended up headless if she had not been pre-warned of the arrest, but doesn't this once again reveal your true character. The truth is you were easily swayed all your life. People who had served you loyally for many years could find themselves in the tower on the flimsiest evidence. All it took was a word from Cromwell, Norfolk or Gardiner. Whether you listened to them depended on your mood which meant their very lives depended on your mood. You were pathetic Henry-a weakling who was easy prey for a manipulative man."

Henry hesitated before answering. Lightfoot had said much the same thing and, while Henry had reacted with rage, his lawyer had made him face the fact that there was some truth in the accusation.

"I will admit that I sometimes should have questioned the motives of some of my councillors when they made allegations. At the time I did not know how devoted to the Protestant cause Thomas Cromwell was. Gardiner was in the opposite camp and I see now that he chose when to drop poison in my ear very wisely. At the time he accused Catherine Parr I was bed-ridden and in pain. I had also recently stated that I hated the drift towards Protestantism in my Church. And of course, Norfolk was always making mischief. But it was never weakness."

"I think it was obviously weakness. You were a weak character Henry but it was more than that. You are a man who totally lacked empathy for your fellow human beings. When you sentenced someone to die you had zero sympathy for them, their children or other family. I don't think you gave them a second thought. You had no understanding of the terror your victims faced. You had a callous disregard for every human life except your own. Is that not true?"

"No, and I sentenced no one. The law did that."

"It was your law Henry as I think we have already made clear. And it is true, as I am sure the jury will agree. It is said that the definition of evil is a complete inability to have any empathy for another's suffering. And this sums you up Henry. You were an evil man and it is only by good fortune that Catherine Parr, who was a gentle, kind woman, did not become another victim of yours."

Before he could reply she turned to the judge.

"That concludes the prosecution's case in regard to Catherine Parr My Lord."

Chapter Twenty

The case against Henry the 8th in regard to Catherine Parr

The Defence

"Henry, when Bishop Gardiner pointed out that the views Catherine expressed to you that night constituted heresy did you agree with him?"

"Yes, I did."

"And thinking back on them now do you still consider them to be so?"

"Yes, if taken at face value."

"And that is my point. When she spoke the words, you thought them heresy. It is only when she explained the context that you viewed them differently. Is that the case?"

"Yes. She explained to me that she was just asking my advice on what constituted heresy."

"So she was looking for guidance from you and the words expressed were not actually her beliefs."

"That is correct."

"So when Gardiner said she had spoken heresy you had no choice but to sign her arrest warrant. And when the context of her words were explained to you, you rescinded that warrant. Is that the case?"

"Yes,"

Lightfoot looked to the juror's bench.

"So, Ladies and Gentlemen of the jury. This is the vengeful, murderous, and cruel Henry the 8th we have heard so much about these past centuries. A charge of

148

heresy was made and after a short explanation this charge was dismissed. The King gave his Queen the benefit of the doubt, something most historians think he was incapable of. We also now know that these were indeed Catherine's views and, at the time, would constitute heresy which was punishable by death."

Lightfoot turned to look back at Henry.

"Henry, did you truly believe Catherine's explanation?"

"I accepted the explanation but I was aware that she was in sympathy with those who wished for more religious reform."

"Would it be fair to say that you wished to believe her?"

"That would be accurate, yes."

"And you wished this because you liked and admired her?"

"Yes."

"I know that in recent days you have read of Catherine's life after your death. Would you now accept that she was much more devoted to the protestant cause than you previously thought?"

"Yes, very much so."

"So, when she spoke to you that night, she almost certainly believed in what she was saying?"

"Yes."

"At the time you and the likes of Bishop Gardiner were trying to rein back from the drift away from the Roman Catholic religion. Some very high profile people, including confidants of the Queen, had been burnt at the stake for expressing Protestant views. Do you think it possible that she was trying to influence your religious views that night- to try to change the direction of travel?"

"Yes, I think that is very possible."

"And have you considered that the very reason that she accepted your marriage proposal was to try to effect this change of policy? She is reported to have said that she felt it her duty to marry you. Now you could take this to mean her duty to her family, her country and her King. But what she might have meant was her duty to the Protestant cause."

"Yes, in recent days I have considered that and I suspect that was at least one reason. I don't believe it was the only one as there was genuine affection between us."

"But even though you accepted her explanation at the time, in your heart of hearts you must have at least suspected that she was not being completely honest. Would that be fair?"

"As you said, I chose to believe her but yes, I suspected she might have meant her words."

"So, you were in effect being merciful?"

"You could put it that way but I prefer to see it as giving her a second chance as I considered her confused."

"To be fair Henry, pretty much everyone in the kingdom must have been confused as to what was official religious doctrine and what was heresy. From the point of your split from Rome it appears to have changed daily."

"That was never my intention. All I wanted was to be the ultimate power in my kingdom as was my God given right. I never intended England to be in any way a supporter of the Protestant cause."

"It might not have been your intention but that is what happened. Everyone, from you yourself, to the lowest peasant was confused and they would continue to be so for centuries. Even in the 21st century the Church of England, that you created, is a hotch-potch. It is supposedly a Protestant country but the interior of most churches differ little from Catholic ones."

"It was Cromwell who set England on this path. I did not know at the time of his Protestant sympathies and I allowed him too much power."

"You did so because allowing him to dissolve the monasteries made you very rich. But the policy deepened your split from Rome and encouraged those with Protestant sympathies. But the point I expect my colleague, the council for the prosecution, to make is this. Why was Catherine Parr allowed to get away with heresy when others were burnt at the stake?"

"I was not convinced of her guilt."

"Yes, you gave her the benefit of the doubt. But would you admit many others did not receive the same benefit?"

"I was not in a position to judge them as I was my wife."

Henry knew this response would anger Lightfoot. He had warned Henry about this line of questioning and had insisted it was necessary as the prosecution would fill the gap if he did not. Henry could understand the logic of this because Amira Hussein's questioning would have been much more aggressive. But it still irked Henry to have to justify himself.

"But does it not lend weight to the accusation that justice in your land was pretty haphazard and depended on influence rather than actual guilt or innocence? Catherine had your backing and continued to live in great splendour as your Queen. At the same time another woman who held the same views might suffer the most horrific death imaginable. It hardly seems fair."

"I cannot deny influence played a part in the law of the land but surely that has always been so and always will be. If you have powerful friends in any level of society you are going to have a better chance under the law. It is not how it should be but it is impossible to stop. Is it really any different in the 21st Century?"

"No, it is not and I personally think it reflects well on you that you gave Catherine the benefit of the doubt. The prosecutions accusation that you were weak to not immediately dismiss Bishop Gardiner's charge of heresy is plainly false. It actually took strength to put aside your personal good feelings for Catherine and to allow her comments to be examined."

Lightfoot turned towards the Jury.

"Ladies and Gentlemen of the jury, it is hard in the modern world to understand heresy charges. But in Henry's time they played a huge part in society. There was an almost universal belief that the devil was active among the people. To be accused of heresy was to be accused of working with the devil.

"It is in this light that Henry's decision to arrest Catherine, and then to dismiss these charges after investigation, should be seen. Henry behaved properly in both cases. The prosecution continues to paint Henry as history has portrayed him but, to my mind, this is just lazy research. I think this trial has highlighted that he tried to uphold the law and was capable of compassion and fairness."

He turned towards the judge.

"The defence in regard to Catherine Parr rests My Lord. I think we have proved that, on this point at least, there is no case to answer."

"Thank you, Mr. Lightfoot. Do you wish to cross-examine Miss Hussein?"

"I just have one point I would like to make to the jury My Lord."

"Very well, go ahead."

Amira Hussein stood up but did not move from behind her desk. She glanced at Henry but then turned to the jury.

"Ladies and Gentlemen of the jury, the council for the defence has painted Henry's decision to have Catherine arrested after Gardiner's heresy charge, and then to retract that arrest, as noble and a sign of strength.

"I am sure that, like me, you find that laughable. Gardiner whispered heresy in his ear, and he believed him. Catherine then whispered words of innocence in the same ear and he then believed her. There was no investigation as the defence claims. Far from being a sign of strength it is unbelievable weakness. It was pathetic and this sort of thing happened all through his reign. He was pathetic. People lived or died a terrible death based on who whispered in his ear last. This is not lazy research. It is cold fact that is supported by Henry's own words."

She turned to the judge.

"The prosecution has nothing more to say on this particular charge My Lord."

Chapter Twenty-One

The case against Henry the 8th in regard to Thomas Cromwell

The Prosecution

"It was reported that soon after Thomas Cromwell's execution you regretted it and blamed others for making false accusations. Is this true?"

Henry looked at her. The woman still intrigued him but he was worried by her confidence and intelligence.

"Yes, it is,"

"So, as I pointed out in the Catherine Parr case, his enemies whispered in your ear and you, rather pathetically, listened to their lies. And in that moment your most loyal and brilliant servant's fate was sealed. The man who had made you rich and freed you from your first marriage didn't even get the chance to explain himself to you as Catherine did."

"They were not exactly lies, not all of them anyway."

"What was he charged with?"

"There were a number of charges, the main ones being treason and heresy."

"So, was he or was he not guilty of both?"

"Under the law at the time he was almost certainly guilty of both."

"So they were not false accusations?"

Henry sighed.

"They were false in that he was not working against me."

"You will have to explain that."

"We now know that he was devoted to the Protestant cause but that was not known at the time. He clearly tried to influence me but, in retrospect, I don't think he went too far. He may have served the Protestant cause as well but I feel his service to me was his priority. Unfortunately, for a short time, I allowed myself to be convinced otherwise."

"A short time in which he was executed."

"Yes, I am afraid so."

"Ok, that covers the heresy charge for the moment but what about the alleged treason?"

"That covered several charges, the two main ones being that he used his position to enrich himself and of plotting to marry Princess Mary, my daughter."

"And you think he was guilty of both?"

"No, I think he was possibly guilty of the first charge but not the second."

"Could you expand on that please?"

"He probably used his high offices to make himself rich. But Cromwell was already a very wealthy lawyer and businessman when he came to serve me. So it is hard to judge. Also, most people in high office abuse their position to make money. People did it in the centuries before my time and I am sure they still do it now. It is basic human nature. Monarchs and leaders turn a blind idea as long as it doesn't cause problems or if it effects the service given to them."

"And this was true of Cromwell. His first priority was to you, and you certainly prospered from following his advice. So what if he made a little money on the side? I am assuming that was your attitude was it not?"

"That would be correct."

"So, it only became a stick to beat him with when he fell out of favour for a time and you allowed his many enemies to brief against him?"

"Unfortunately, you are again correct. Norfolk and the others convinced me that Cromwell was working against me, the church and the country."

"And they also convinced you he was plotting to marry the Princess Mary-that he intended to make himself King?"

"This was a rumour that had been going round court for several years. I had even laughed at the absurdity of the charge along with Cromwell. I think it possible he may once, as he rose to prominence, have thought about it but he would never have acted on that impulse. He knew me well enough to know that I would never have allowed it."

"But again, when the charge was laid against him, you did not argue against it?"

"No, I did not. Cromwell's enemies chose their moment well. I was unhappy with Cromwell and I allowed myself to be convinced that he was capable of any crime."

"Why were you unhappy with him?"

"He had arranged and encouraged my marriage to Anne of Cleves. He said it was to gain an important ally in Europe. But the circumstances changed, and this alliance would not have been needed. I felt he should have foreseen this."

"It is also claimed that he, along with the painter Holbein, misrepresented her appearance. Is that true?"

"The painting was indeed flattering to the Lady and I thought at the time Cromwell had encouraged Holbein to do so. On reflection I think both men probably acted in good faith."

"But did you think that Cromwell had an ulterior motive for promoting the match?"

"The Duke of Norfolk, Stephen Gardiner and others believed it was because she was Protestant. They alleged that Cromwell wanted the marriage because it might persuade me to more reform of my church."

"And you believed them?"

"Yes and, knowing what I know now, I was almost certainly right to do so. But I came to believe, regrettably too late, that Cromwell would have put my interests above his own. At the time I had many powerful enemies in Europe and I think his priority was to gain an ally."

"And was the Anne of Cleves marriage the only reason for his fall from favour?"

"No. I was unhappy with a lot of the more radical changes in the church as were most of the nobility. I also come to the conclusion that he had got too arrogant and that his unpopularity in both the court and the country was causing problems."

"So he had got too big for his boots and needed taking down a peg or two."

"It is not how I would have put it but he had become increasingly disrespectful to other members of the council."

"You mean the Duke of Norfolk and other members of the nobility specifically?"

"Yes,"

"But is it not true that they had been laying charges of disrespect and arrogance against him for years. Why did you now decide to take heed of them?"

"Like I said, they chose their moment well. I was displeased with Cromwell, and they took advantage."

"Ok, I can accept that the disastrous Anne of Cleves marriage, and Cromwell's role in it, played a part. But is it not true that Cromwell was doomed from the start?"

"No, of course not."

"I think it is. The truth is that you always saw him as Norfolk and the others saw him. He was the upstart son of a blacksmith who got above his station. You protected him from the nobility because you were smart enough to appreciate his talents. But as soon as he failed you, even once, he was finished. Is that not the truth of it?"

"I regretted his death and you are right in that I was too easily swayed by others. But his background played no part in the decision to charge him with treason. I enjoyed his company, conversation and intelligence."

"But you were never friends, were you? You never saw him as your equal?"

"I was a King. I saw no one as an equal."

"That is a revealing statement but let us go back a little bit. All through this trial I have made the point that justice in your kingdom, especially among those in your court, was arbitrary. Guilt or innocence pretty much depended on your mood or being in or out of your favour. Doesn't the Thomas Cromwell execution provide ample evidence that this was true?"

"No, it does not. Cromwell was condemned by the law and, as I have pointed out, he was guilty of treasonous crimes."

"You have also pointed out that you were aware of these treasonous crimes for several years but turned a blind eye as he was a great help to you. When he annoyed you these crimes suddenly mattered. Doesn't this prove that justice depended on your good favour?"

"You are twisting my words."

"I did not twist them. They are in the court records. You said, "Monarchs and leaders turn a blind eye as long as it doesn't cause problems or effects the service given to them." I can have the court clerk read them back to you if you like."

"That will not be necessary."

"So, do you accept that your anger at him was the driving force behind his arrest and execution. Do you accept that neither would have happened if you had not been angry with him?"

"It was more complicated than that. The heresy charges were more important, and it cannot be argued that he did not desire the country to move to the Protestant cause. In the end he pushed on this too far and when Norfolk and the others pointed this out it was impossible for me to disagree."

"But again, I think you must have known that Cromwell favoured moving the church further from the Roman Catholic doctrine. While you did not know the extent he was committed to it, or about his Protestant contacts, you had to be aware that he favoured change. Had he not once passed you a bible published in English?"

"Yes, he did."

"And was that not considered heresy at the time?"

"Yes, it was."

"And what did you do when he showed it to you?"

Henry sighed in resignation.

"I did nothing,"

"So you allowed blatant heresy to go unchecked?"

"At the time allowing the Bible to be printed in English seemed to make sense to me."

"So did that make you a heretic?"

"Look, I had recently split from Rome. There was a lot of confusion about what was heresy."

"Which is exactly my point. It was not considered heresy at that time as Cromwell was in your good books. Later, when he fell out of favour, it was heresy and he ended up dead. As I have said many times, this was the story of your reign. At the highest level the law was just a sham. It was all about what mood you were in."

"That is a false impression."

"You keep saying that but the evidence does not in any way support you. Tell me this, if you had decided earlier that the charges against Cromwell were false would he have been executed?"

"No, of course not."

"Why not? Had he not been found guilty?"

"As I am sure you know Cromwell was not put on trial. I authorised my parliament to bring a bill of attainder against him and the bill was passed."

"So the bill passed, which is not entirely surprising since you had brought it before your own parliament. So what would have happened if you had changed your mind?"

"I suppose I would have brought another bill overruling the first one. I am not sure of the legal process."

"Well, I don't suppose you were but what did it matter anyway? If you had wanted Cromwell to die, he would die. If you wanted him to live he would have lived. Is that not the truth?"

"I was the King and I always had the right to pardon somebody. That was written into the law."

Amira Hussein paused at this.

"You make a good and valid point Henry. Yes, you had the right but why then was Cromwell not pardoned?"

Henry hesitated, knowing she had trapped him.

"The case against him, as Norfolk and the others put it to me, was strong and I didn't feel it was right to pardon him."

"But later you came to believe they had over-egged the case against him and made false charges. If you had had the chance would you have then pardoned him?"

"Yes, I would have."

"But by then you had come to realise what a loss to you he was going to be. Is that true?"

"Yes,"

"You have blamed Norfolk and the others enough. Let us be clear about this. You turned on Cromwell because he had angered you by forcing the Anne of Cleves marriage on you. He had also angered you in matters of religion and several other things. You allowed him to be charged with treason because you were angry with him. And you didn't save him from the headsman because you were still angry with him. Everyone in this court knows that is the truth as does anyone with the slightest grasp of history. Can you not admit that it is true?"

Henry paused before answering.

"I do not deny it."

Now Amira Hussein paused.

"So, you do not deny it. I will admit your honesty on this point does surprise me, but it does beg the question of how many others died as a result of your negative emotions. It also suggests that my claim that your trials were a sham are valid does it not?"

"That is not the case."

"I am convinced it is Henry as are about a million historians. For Cromwell you can read Anne Boleyn and her five alleged lovers. Young, stupid Catherine Howard could have been pardoned but your anger ensured she would be executed. And Catherine Parr only survived because she had the chance to calm your anger. That was how random life and death was in your court. It was all down to what mood you were in. And this made you a monster Henry Tudor. Can you not see that even now?"

Henry hesitated as he had no ready answer. He stared at the woman who looked calmly back at him.

"I made mistakes, and my anger played a part in those mistakes, but I respected the law."

"But would you not accept that you were above the law?"

"No, I would not accept that. I had the power to pardon people but I had to abide by the law. "

Amira Hussein gave him a sad, not unfriendly, smile before continuing in a gentle voice.

"But would you now accept Henry that those who you appointed to enforce the law saw you as above it?"

Henry looked at her and knew he had lost the argument and along with it, probably his soul.

"Yes, I would accept that although that was never my intention. I am not and was not a monster."

Amira Hussein looked at the judge.

"I have no further questions at this point My Lord."

Chapter Twenty-Two

The case against Henry the 8th regarding Thomas Cromwell

The Defence

"Ladies and Gentlemen of the jury, Thomas Cromwell was guilty of the crimes he was accused of. That should not be forgotten. Because of that fact his execution should play no part in the proceedings against Henry Tudor. Throughout this trial the prosecution has accused Henry of making the legal system in his time a sham. But no such accusation can be made in this case. No serious historian believes that Cromwell didn't use his position to further the Protestant cause. He was guilty of heresy and that carried the death penalty."

Lightfoot walked along the jury bench and then looked back at Henry before continuing.

"By 1540 Thomas Cromwell knew Henry better than anyone. He knew how malleable he was and how easily he could be influenced. He knew, despite being Henry's chief advisor, how fragile his position was. He knew he was hated and feared by pretty much everyone at court. He knew his high office depended solely on the King's continued support. He would also have known that withdrawal of that support would mean, not just a fall from grace, but the end of his life.

"But, Ladies and Gentlemen of the jury, he couldn't stop himself. Cromwell had hugely angered the King over his handling of the Anne of Cleves marriage. Henry had been humiliated. To get an annulment he had to confess he had not managed to get an erection on their wedding night so the marriage had not been consummated. For any man that would have to be excruciating but to a medieval King, who knew he had to portray strength and virility to survive, it must have been doubly so.

"But Henry did not immediately order Cromwell's arrest. Within months he was even promoted to the station of Earl of Essex. But Cromwell must have known that he was much weakened at court and that his enemies were whispering poison into the Kings ear. But he could have survived. He was much smarter than his rivals and the fact that he survived the Anne of Cleves debacle suggested that Henry knew his value.

But he didn't backtrack on his policy of the reformation of the Church even though he knew the pace of change, as well as its huge unpopularity, worried the King. The policy had caused near rebellion and Henry had distanced himself from Cromwell as a result. But Cromwell continued despite this. He even sanctioned the destruction of the monastery that contained the bodies of the Duke of Norfolk's ancestors. His most deadly rival had to have them dug up and replaced in his family vault. Considering this occurred at the time he was losing his influence with the King it amounts to an act of near insanity.

"So why did he do it? That arrogance played a part I do not doubt but Cromwell had a brilliant mind. In his younger years it is probable that he met with Niccolo Macchiavelli and he had shown skills that master of human cunning would have been proud of. Cromwell had been like a chess grand-master in his rise to power so why did he make such terrible moves at the very time he could least afford to?

"I think the answer lies in what we now know were Cromwell's religious convictions. At the time it was known that he had some sympathy with the new religion but no one could have guessed how committed to the cause he was. There is very good evidence that he used his position to protect high-profile Protestants who had been condemned as heretics.

"He also took massive risks in his private conversations with the King. We know he gave him a copy of the bible printed in English. This was heresy and if Henry had reacted badly Cromwell would have been arrested on the spot. Some people have claimed Henry the 8th was England's first Protestant King. This is false. Henry died as a Catholic. But Cromwell, with enormous courage and cunning, convinced him to abandon some of the Catholic doctrine and take up a few of the Protestant teachings.

"I believe it is quite possible that England would not have become a Protestant country without the efforts of Thomas Cromwell. After both Katherine of Aragon and Anne Boleyn had died it is feasible that Henry could have patched up his differences with the Pope and returned England to the Catholic fold. But Cromwell, who was then at the hight of his powers, would have done everything he could to have prevented this.

"Cromwell's decision to promote the marriage to Anne of Cleves is further evidence of this. There is no doubt it would have benefited Henry at the time as it gave him a powerful European ally. But I suspect Cromwell had an ulterior motive. What was most important to him was that Anne of Cleves was a Protestant as were her powerful family. Henry's marriage to a Protestant would have prevented any reconciliation with the Pope.

"But after the marriage proved to be a disaster, along with the King removing his favour, Cromwell must have at least suspected he was on decidedly dodgy ground. So why did he not backtrack and ride out the storm. As I have said, he was far cleverer than his enemies. He could have got back in favour.

"But I also believe he was smart enough to know that he would never have the power he had before. He would never have the influence over Henry he once had. And that would mean the religious direction of travel would slow and probably even reverse. Henry, under the influence of people like Norfolk and Bishop Gardiner, could have taken England back to Rome.

"And this is why I think Cromwell did not change course. This is why he, in the last few weeks of his life, did everything he possibly could to hasten the pace of change. Even though he probably knew it would cost him his life he wanted to make it as hard as possible for the Catholics to reverse the changes. In a way he became a martyr for the Protestant cause."

Lightfoot looked at Henry who looked somewhat stunned.

"Knowing what you know now do you think that is a possible explanation for Cromwell's actions Henry?"

"Yes...Yes, I do. It all makes sense now."

"Why did Cromwell not receive a trial?"

Henry looked and felt embarrassed

"He was a brilliant lawyer, the best in the land. It was felt that he could mount a credible defence."

"That hardly seems fair Henry."

"It was not fair."

"Was that your idea?"

"No, that was down to Norfolk and the others."

"But you allowed it?"

"Yes, I did,"

"I want you to be honest now Henry. What was the main reason why Cromwell was executed?"

"There were a number of reasons but the main one was his unpopularity in the land. He was hated and this was proving dangerous to my reign. There had already been armed rebellions."

"But he had always been unpopular."

"Yes, but his brilliant works had made him a huge asset. It was a balancing act. For a time I could put up with his unpopularity but it eventually became very dangerous. When that happened he became a liability."

"I can understand that but surely you can see why people would condemn you for this. It was a betrayal of a loyal servant. And you made him a scape-goat as he was only implementing your policies. You would rather him be hated than you. He was happy to fill this role and his only thanks was the axe."

"Yes, I can understand that."

"But, having said all that, Cromwell was not entirely innocent was he? Under the laws of the time he was guilty of heresy and, to some degree at least, probably guilty of using his office to enrich himself."

"Yes,"

"And many men had been executed for far less?"

"Yes,"

"But you regretted his death, and you wish you had pardoned him?"

"Yes, I did. He was a brilliant man and a loyal servant."

"For how long had the Duke of Norfolk and others been persuading you that Cromwell was guilty of treason and heresy?"

"From the very first moment I showed him favour. It got worse after he arranged my divorce from Catherine of Aragon."

"So that would be over four years?"

"Yes,"

"And, knowing what you know now, do you think he was technically guilty for all that time?"

"He would have certainly been guilty of heresy from the beginning."

Lightfoot turned towards the jury.

"So you see Ladies and Gentlemen of the jury, Henry wasn't the man most responsible for Thomas Cromwell's execution. That honour would fall to Cromwell himself.

"Henry had given him more leeway than he had any man. He had ignored heresy and the allegations of corruption. He had done so because he knew Cromwell's value to him. But Cromwell pushed too hard. We now know he was a committed Protestant and in trying to further that cause he over-reached himself.

"It has long been claimed that Henry turned against him for a number of reasons. They are all justified. Henry was angry at the Anne of Cleves debacle. He was also concerned by the pace of change in his Church. And of course Cromwell's unpopularity in the land had resulted in open rebellion against the crown.

"But, while the execution does not reflect well on Henry, Cromwell knew the dangers of his actions. He knew how fragile his position was. He knew he was just one burst of Henry's temper away from oblivion.

"Of course, Norfolk and his other enemies played a part. But, while they embellished and exaggerated his crimes, there was an element of truth in their accusations. And that is my point. Cromwell had transgressed the heresy laws at least. He gave his enemies a chance to destroy him, and they did. All they had to do was wait for him to anger and disappoint the King.

"The truth is Cromwell played the game. He had an opportunity to further the Protestant cause in England, along with his own personal ambitions, and he took it. But in doing so he broke the law as it was at the time and paid the price.

"And we should not be too sympathetic as Cromwell had played a part in the deaths of several others who were probably far more innocent than he was. He played the game very well but in the end he over-played his hand and lost. And while Henry could have pardoned him he was under no obligation to do so. I say again. Henry was not responsible for Cromwell's death."

He turned to the judge.

"That concludes the defence in regard to Thomas Cromwell my Lord."

The judge nodded.

"Thank you, Mr. Lightfoot. Do you have anything to add Miss Hussein?"

"Yes, I just have one question for the defendant."

She stood up but did not move from behind her desk.

"Henry, you have stated that the principal reason for Cromwell's arrest and execution was down to his unpopularity in the land. You claim that this unpopularity was becoming dangerous and might ultimately be a threat to your reign. Is this correct?"

"Yes, it is,"

"So, in effect you had him killed to protect your position. You had the man who had solved so many problems for you killed to save your own skin. You had a faithful servant killed to placate an angry mob. You placed all the blame for your all the policies you were ultimately responsible for on him. Would that be a fair assessment?"

"It would be grossly unfair."

"Please explain to me why it is unfair."

"Cromwell came up with the policies and, while I permitted him to go ahead with them, he went further than I had agreed to."

"So, you are saying the hatred people had for him was his own fault and in no part due to obeying your orders?"

Henry hesitated.

"No...No... Okay, I have to accept some responsibility but it is the truth that Cromwell exceeded my orders on many occasions."

"But you have stated that the main reason that he was killed was his unpopularity. Do you not concede that having him executed eased the pressure on you? Do you not concede that having him executed meant that, in effect, he was to blame for all the unpopular policies?"

Henry again hesitated before looking her squarely in the eye.

"No, I do not concede that."

Amira Hussein turned and smiled at the jury before looking at the judge.

"I have no further questions my Lord."

Chapter Twenty-Three

Final arguments
The Prosecution

"Ladies and Gentlemen of the jury, sometimes history does not truly represent a man. There are several reasons for this, one being that history is written by the victors in a war. This is often cited in the case of Richard the Third who was defeated and killed by the forces of Henry's father in the war of the roses.

"History's very negative view of Richard is largely influenced by the writings of William Shakespeare. The problem with this of course, is that Shakespeare wrote his play about Richard during the reign of Henry's daughter, Elizabeth. I doubt our William would have been stupid enough to paint Richard as a hero and rightful King as this would have made her grand-father and, by extension herself, a usurper.

"There are numerous other examples. In the United States of America George Washington is viewed almost as a saint. He was the noblest man who ever lived and legend has it that he never told a lie. The problem with this is that Washington owned hundreds of slaves and no one in history ever got to the top in politics without lying.

"But this positive view of Washington serves a purpose. It helped build a country. The legend helped generations of Americans see themselves, and their country, embodying the supposed virtues of its first president. When the legend becomes fact, print the legend."

Henry watched from the dock as Amira Hussein paused and glanced at him before once again addressing the jury.

"But, Ladies and Gentlemen of the jury, in both these cases you can read the counter arguments. Throughout most of the last five centuries the majority of the literature about Richard the Third has been negative. But there has always been a sizeable minority that have tried to defend him and to cast doubt on the Tudor's version of history.

"Outside of the United States George Washington is seen in a more realistic light. Even in the States you will find historians willing to push the argument that he, while undoubtedly a great man, had feet of clay."

She turned once more to look at Henry for a moment before continuing.

"But, Ladies and Gentlemen of the jury, it is very different where Henry the 8th of England is concerned. Henry, like Richard the 3rd, is viewed as a psychopathic monster. But, unlike Richard, it is very hard to find, in the whole of history, anyone prepared to contradict this view. Hardly anyone has tried to defend him or change the narrative. The last person to do so was his daughter Elizabeth, and, considering she wore a closed ring containing the image of her executed mother for all her life, we may assume she was only playing lip-service when she did so.

"Catholics understandably hate him but even strict Protestants do so as well. Have any of you, in all honesty, ever read a book or seen a movie that didn't portray him as a selfish self-obsessed murderer of his wives, ministers, servants and even friends?

"Have any of you ever watched a movie and been persuaded that yes, of course Anne Boleyn would have been insane enough to sleep with three of his best friends, a servant and even her own brother? No, of course you haven't as no movie-maker, historian or novelist has ever seriously tried to do so."

Amira Hussein looked once more at Henry before walking to the centre of the room and turning back to the jury.

"And there is a good reason for this. There is one simple reason, and that one reason is this. It is because it is beyond doubt that Henry the 8th was a self-obsessed murderer of his wives, ministers, servants and even friends. To defend him there has to be some evidence to the contrary. A defence has to be built on evidential foundations and there is none.

"That is not to say there is no evidence. There is plenty of evidence. The English are great at keeping archive material, especially when it comes to the nobility. There are numerous court and parliament records. There are private and public correspondence between the main players in this drama. There are letters and memoirs from foreign ambassadors and fellow monarchs. Oh yes, there is plenty of evidence but, unfortunately for Henry, it pretty much all supports the view history has of him."

She walked slowly towards the jury as she continued.

"No, Ladies and Gentlemen of the jury, history has not misrepresented Henry the 8th of England. In this case at least, history has got it absolutely right. It has judged Henry a monster and no one, the defence included, can reasonably argue against that judgment.

"They will try of course. They have already done so. They argue that Henry followed the law at all times. They would have us believe that it was a court of law that found Anne Boleyn and her supposed army of lovers guilty of capital crimes. And of course it was parliament that did for Thomas Cromwell. It is bunkum Ladies and Gentlemen. None of these people would have died if Henry had wanted them to live. Henry was not just above the law; he was the law.

"Catherine of Aragon was divorced and kept a prisoner for the rest of her life because Henry willed it so. Anne Boleyn and five others were executed because Henry wanted out of his second marriage. Six people died for the simple, and very selfish, reason that Henry had discovered that mistresses don't make great wives. Catherine Howard was a silly star-struck child but Henry was to show no mercy while Catherine Parr just got lucky.

"And on top of all this were all the ministers and councillors who were killed. Nearly all of them had served him faithfully for years but their loyalty was so often rewarded with the axe. Thomas Cromwell and Thomas More were the most high-profile but there were dozens more. Cardinal Wolsey had bent over backwards to try to get the Pope to grant an annulment of Henry's first marriage. But all he got for his troubles was an accusation of treason. Only his premature death saved him from execution."

Amira Hussein paused and looked at Henry. She locked eyes with him for several seconds before turning back to the jury.

"Ladies and Gentlemen of the jury, these are the actions of a very evil man. I fail to see how any right-minded person can argue with that statement. The defence can bring up legal technicalities. They can mention that a King in Henry's time had almost limitless powers. They can even mention the fact that a few of his victims may have been technically guilty.

"But none of that matters much. None of that can disguise the fact that Henry behaved like a monster. He is nothing less than a mass murderer. People, quite understandably, lived in terror of him and he revelled in it. You could be his loyal friend one day and a headless traitor the next. No one was safe.

"It is occasionally argued that, as it took Henry seven years to attain a divorce from Catherine of Aragon, that this proves he respected the law. A very small minority suggest that, because she wasn't falsely accused of treason and executed it means Henry would never countenance such an act. It is even suggested that this means Anne Boleyn was guilty of treason or else she would have just been divorced as Catherine was.

"This is nonsense. It is baloney. Catherine of Aragon was only spared the axe because Henry knew that it would mean war with both Spain and the Pope if she wasn't'"

"THAT IS A DAMNED LIE," screamed Henry as he stood up. "There was never a question of Catherine being tried for treason. She was never in danger of execution, never, do you hear me?"

Amira Hussein looked at him calmly as the judge rebuked him.

"Sir. You must remain silent at this point of the proceedings. Your council will have a chance to challenge the prosecutions assertions later. But, for now, you must allow Miss Hussein to continue."

Henry looked at him. He was livid.

"But she should not be allowed to lie like that. That was a pure falsehood."

"As I said, your council will have ample time to make that point. Mr Lightfoot can you please advise your client."

Lightfoot stood up.

"Yes, your honour. Henry, please remain silent. I will have my time and your protests will be heard and your position defended."

Henry glared at him before conceding the point.

"Very well. I shall remain silent as I listen to these outrageous lies."

Amira Hussein nodded at the judge and looked blankly at Henry before turning back to the jury.

"But Anne Boleyn had no such protection. No foreign nation was going to threaten war if she was executed. She did not even have the support of the general public who hated her for usurping their beloved Catherine and causing the break with the Catholic church. No, Anne Boleyn could be disposed of with no fear of reprisals.

"And this is what Henry did. I have no doubt Thomas Cromwell played his part and he may have taken the opportunity to settle a few personal scores with Norris, Brereton, and Weston. But Henry was ultimately responsible for all the deaths. Cromwell may not have received a direct order but he would not have acted without knowing he would have Henry's approval.

"Henry sanctioned their deaths. If he had not done so they would not have died. That is the simple truth. Did he honestly believe Anne was guilty of adultery and treason? Yes, I believe he did but Norris, Brereton, and Weston? No, in his heart of hearts he must have at least suspected that they were innocent. But he did nothing to save them. They were his loyal friends of many years but he let them die because he knew that not to do so would cast doubt on Anne's guilt. Ladies and Gentlemen of the jury, is that not truly evil?

"Catherine Howard was a seventeen-year-old. She had been used by powerful older men all her miserable life.

She had almost certainly been sexually abused by at least one of them. And when she attracted the attention of the most powerful man of them all her fate was sealed.

"She had no choice but to marry him. Her father and uncle made sure of that. Was she guilty of the charges made against her? Quite possibly but others were much more guilty. She was a pawn in men's plans and had little or no choice to go along with them. She was manipulated and almost certainly blackmailed. And Henry must have been aware of this.

"But that did not save her. There was no compassion in Henry Tudor's heart. There was not a trace of sympathy for a teenage girl who was in way above her head and had no choice but to be so. Ladies and Gentlemen of the jury, how could any man who knew the poor girls background and how she had been manipulated and used, still send her to the execution block? Can such a person not be described as anything other than irredeemably evil?

"And what of her lady-in-waiting, Lady Rochford? When she was declared insane and mentally unfit to stand trial Henry just bypassed the law and had her executed anyway. Ladies and Gentlemen of the jury, anytime the defence makes the claim that Henry always acted in accordance with the law, and they have made that claim many times already, remember Lady Rochford's fate.

"And remember too that Catherine Howard was convicted of breaking a law that didn't even exist at the time. It was created by Henry's tame parliament two months after the act to ensure no escape from the block. It was an obscenity that makes a mockery of Henry's claim to respect the law. Henry the 8th was above the law. That would be obvious to a ten-year-old school child studying history for the first time. It would be clear to them within an hour that Henry was an all-powerful dictator.

"No, Henry Tudor cannot use the law in his defence. Such a claim would be laughable if it wasn't so sick. The law was for Henry's subjects but not for him. He abided by it when it suited him and ignored it when it didn't."

She paused and locked eyes with every member of the jury for several seconds. She glanced at Henry and then walked back to her desk before turning towards the jury again.

"Ladies and Gentlemen of the jury, the punishment if Henry is found guilty today is severe. His soul will burn in hell for all eternity and no effort will be made to repair his reputation. All men and women are ultimately judged. There is always an accounting. You may get away with a crime in your own life-time but there will always be a reckoning.

"But only a limited number face what Henry faces if found guilty. It is a very high bar set by the likes of Hitler, Stalin and Genghis Khan. So why is Henry in danger of such a fate? The three I have mentioned murdered millions while even his harshest critic would not accuse Henry of more than twenty at the most. I would suggest that the word "Murder" could only, in all fairness, be used six or seven times.

"So why is he here? Why does he deserve to face the same fate as Adolf Hitler who unleashed upon the world the most destructive war in history- a war that would leave more than twenty million people dead. Hitler was the man chiefly responsible for a holocaust that left six million people, most of them Jewish, dead. Surely Henry's crimes, if they are crimes, fade into insignificance when measured against such horror."

Amira Hussein paused and once again made eye contact with all the jurors. Henry had to admire her sense of theatre. It was working as well as every eye in the court was on her. Henry felt oppressed and cowed by the incredible tension in the room.

"I will tell you why Ladies and Gentlemen of the jury. It is because of the casual disregard for human life. Men and women were sentenced to death when he must have known they were almost certainly innocent.

"It is because he changed the religion of a country for the most selfish of reasons. This caused terror among millions of his subjects who had the impossible choice of following his direction or risking death by, in their eyes, staying loyal to God. It is hard for us to understand in the modern world how faith in God was central to everything in the 1500's.

"But, make no mistake, many would have seen following Henry's orders as a risk to their mortal soul. How many were burnt at the stake for choosing God over King? All of these deaths can be attributed to Henry Tudor. And they didn't end with his death. For nearly 500 years Catholics and Protestants in the British Isles, especially Ireland, have been slaughtering each other. Those countless deaths, and they continue to this day, can also be added to Henry's tally.

"Ladies and Gentlemen of the jury, being a King means you have great power but it also brings great responsibility. Henry had a responsibility to care for his subjects and he spread terror amongst them. He had a responsibility to uphold the law but he made a mockery of it. He had a responsibility to uphold the Catholic faith but he undermined it to suit himself. He had a responsibility to his friends but he betrayed them and had some executed. And he had a responsibility to his wives but he betrayed and imprisoned one and executed two."

She again paused. She looked at Henry, the judge and Lightfoot before turning back to the jury.

"Ladies and Gentlemen of the jury. Henry the 8th of England fully deserves his fate. His crimes have echoed down through 450 years of history. People still die because of his actions. He was an evil man who refused to show mercy to those who had served and loved him for years."

She turned and walked back to her chair. Before sitting down she again looked at the jury.

"Ladies and Gentlemen of the jury, I urge you to find him guilty and to do the same. There should be no mercy for Henry Tudor."

Chapter Twenty-Four

Final Arguments
The Defence

Lightfoot stood up and then walked slowly along the jury bench making eye contact with all jurors. He then walked back to the centre of the room before looking at Henry and the judge before once more turning towards the jury.

"Ladies and Gentlemen of the jury, towards the end of his reign and life Henry the 8th of England was a very unpleasant man. He was ruthless, merciless, selfish, completely lacking in empathy and often cruel.

"But ladies and Gentlemen of the jury, he was not a 16th century Adolf Hitler or Genghis Khan. His supposed crimes, and it is arguable if they were crimes at all, were in no way comparable to those of Josef Stalin. Ladies and Gentlemen of the jury, Henry the 8th of England was not a monster.

"Breaking with the Church of Rome, and essentially changing the religion of England, just to get a divorce was selfish in the extreme. It caused terror among his people and led to centuries of violence and countless deaths. But he could not have foreseen these consequences. Kings and Presidents make decisions that reverberate down the centuries. But no man can predict the future and it would be grossly unfair, and frankly ridiculous, to lay the blame for sectarian murders in 1980's Northern Ireland at Henry's door.

"Henry's view at the time was simply that a King should be the ultimate power in his land. That might offend modern day republicans but would it not seem reasonable in the 1500's? And it should be remembered that it was all done lawfully.

"It seems very cruel to have cast aside Catherine of Aragon. They had loved each other and she had schooled him in the art of Kingship. In the early part of his reign Henry had been a successful and popular monarch loved by his people. And a lot of the credit for this should go to Catherine.

"But, unfortunately for her, she failed to do the one thing that was absolutely essential for the wife of a King. She was a fantastic Queen in every other respect but she failed the number one requirement. She did not give birth to a male heir.

"We can condemn Henry but consider the choice he had. He could stay loyal to Catherine but that would mean the end of the Tudor line. All his Father had fought for would be gone. It would have been unthinkable. In reality there was no choice. He had to marry again and so he had to divorce Catherine. It was cruel and heartless, but it had to be done if he wanted to continue the Tudor line.

"We can also condemn the way he treated Catherine after the divorce. It seems very harsh to place any blame on her but it is beyond doubt that she brought some of this onto herself. If she had recognised Henry's absolute need to have a legitimate son they could have parted on good terms. If this had been the case Henry would have almost certainly kept her in considerable comfort, and upheld her status in the land, for the rest of her life. A grateful Henry would have tried hard to grant her every wish. We have only to look at his fine treatment of Anne of Cleves after their short marriage to confirm this.

"But Catherine chose to defy him for many years and in those years Henry became very bitter. By the time he eventually freed himself he resented her and was in a mood to punish her. And this he did. It was horrible how he treated her and not letting her see her daughter for most of the rest of her life was vindictive in the extreme.

"But does this make Henry a monster comparable to Adolf Hitler? No, of course it doesn't. Hitler was the devil incarnate who was responsible for the murder of many millions. Henry was just an imbittered ex-husband.

"And, while there is little doubt that his actions were primarily driven by personal bitterness, there were valid reasons for keeping Catherine imprisoned and denying her daughter visitation rights. Catherine was a devout Catholic as was her daughter. Although there is zero evidence that either plotted against the King, both would have been figureheads for the many in the country who did. If they had been allowed to, these Catholic rebels would have approached Catherine in the same way they later approached Mary, Queen of Scots, in the reign of Henry's daughter, Elizabeth.

"So, while we can rightly condemn Henry for the treatment of a once loyal and loving wife, we must also recognise there were legitimate practical reasons for his actions. This of course does not mean we should forgive his behaviour. But are we really to consider it behaviour worthy of eternal damnation? Personally I find the idea ridiculous. He was just a man who, out of both necessity and personal vindictiveness, treated his ex-wife very badly."

Lightfoot walked slowly round the court-room and then looked at Henry for several seconds. Henry looked back at him, not knowing if he was pleased or angry at his lawyer's defence. And then Lightfoot again turned to the jury.

"And so to Anne Boleyn. The execution of his second wife and her alleged lovers is the principal reason that Henry is facing this trial. It is one of the most famous dramas in history. It is a story packed with intrigue, deceit and betrayal. But what makes it so compelling is the unanswered question. Was Anne Boleyn guilty?

"Now countless novels, TV dramas and movies have almost always suggested that no, she wasn't. But novelists and movie makers have a tried and tested formula. They don't want to confuse their audience too much. They like black and white. They also like good and bad guys and, as history has condemned Henry as a very bad guy, they have seen no reason to challenge that theory.

"But serious historians see things very differently. They read surviving court documents and letters. They study the charges and the laws of the time. They look at all the evidence available and the possible motivation of the major players.

"But, even after the most exhaustive research, the honest ones will admit that they can't be sure. They can only offer an informed opinion. We know a lot but not enough to answer one of the most famous and intriguing questions in history: Was Anne Boleyn guilty of adultery?

"Now the majority say no. They, as we have all been conditioned to for centuries, believe she would have been insane to commit adultery. In the close knit world of the court, and with her having so many powerful enemies, it would almost certainly be discovered. To many they were all trumped up charges that would enable Henry to get rid of her and replace her with Jane Seymour. It was a sham trial: A kangaroo court with a pre-determined outcome.

"It is a very powerful argument but it is not one accepted by all historians. There is a sizeable minority that say no, hang on, she may well have been guilty. They base their argument on evidence given under oath, letters between significant characters, overheard conversations and the desperate need of Anne to have a son.

"It is this last that is the most intriguing. Of all the charges laid against Anne the most absurd has always been that she committed incest with her own brother, George. It seems ludicrous and designed to paint Anne as completely vile and as pretty much a witch. This would make her execution popular among the people and stop anyone questioning the validity of the other charges against her. It would also have the bonus of avoiding the embarrassing situation of having George Boleyn in high office after the execution of his sister. Thomas Cromwell has always been seen as the architect of the plan and if so he was very successful.

"But is it such a ridiculous charge? The Boleyn family was very wealthy but they owed their prominence at court, and in the country, solely to the fact Anne was married to the King. George was a member of the privy council and an ambassador. He owed it all to his sister's marriage and if that marriage failed he would surely fall from favour and, in Tudor England, falling from favour often led to execution.

"Is it so implausible that they might have considered passing off a male son conceived between them as the Kings? So what if the child resembled George? It would just be considered that he had inherited more of the Boleyn genes than the Tudor ones.

"Surviving letters between Anne and her brother suggest a closeness and affection that was life-long and unusual in regard to siblings. Letters from others also remark upon it. And let us not forget that during the crucial period of adolescence Anne was living in France and did not see her brother for a long period. Is it not at least possible that their feelings for each other got confused during this time?

"I suspect that, on balance, most would still consider sexual union between them unlikely but surely it cannot be dismissed. And consider the desperation of both. Anne Boleyn needed a son to stay Queen and George needed a nephew to retain his position at court. And both would have considered the possibility of execution if that son did not arrive. Given all that can anyone truly say they were 100% innocent of the charge of adultery?

"The same can be said of the other alleged lovers. The three court gentlemen Norris, Weston and Brereton. Norris especially, was said to be obsessed with the Queen and she no doubt enjoyed the power she had over him. All three fawned over her and she and they flirted outrageously. I am sure everybody in this court room knows of times when flirtation has over-stepped the mark and led to cheating, adultery and marriage break-up.

"But many people counter this argument by saying that the three men would never have had sexual relations with the Queen as it was likely to be discovered and lead to their execution. But would they have been so sensible?

"When it comes to sex even the most sensible men do incredibly stupid things. How many powerful politicians over the years have self-destructed by having illicit affairs? Some take incredible risks. I remember one who, just after being appointed to one of the highest posts in the land, cheated on his wife with a street-walking prostitute.

"The fact that some people who, when having sex, are turned on by the possible chance of discovery is something that has long been recognised by psychologists. We have all heard of the mile-high-club."

Henry saw the jury laugh at this although he had no idea what his council was going on about. Lightfoot waited for the laughter to die down before continuing.

"These were also powerful men and power is an aphrodisiac. These three men had also been born into eminent noble families. They would have had servants, estate workers and the general public doffing their caps to them all of their lives. It would likely to have left them with a massive sense of entitlement. It would probably have made them very arrogant too.

"It is often stated that they were long-term friends of the King even from childhood. But could you really have genuine friendship with a Tudor prince who was to become King? And, while they were still relatively young and virile, Henry was, at this stage, overweight, prematurely aged, and practically an invalid. Would they not have secretly laughed at him?

"It is also suggested that Henry, as a result of his health problems, often suffered from impotence. This can only be speculation but I am sure most modern day doctors would agree that this would be highly likely given his failing health.

"So, given Anne's desperation to bear a son, is it impossible to imagine that at least one of these flirtations went way too far and became adulterous?

"And maybe it wasn't just about bearing a child that could be passed off as the Kings. Anne liked the company of men. She liked the power she had over them. Even before she became Queen men had been falling at her feet. She undoubtedly knew how to tease and enchant men.

"Maybe she went too far. And consider this. She was married to an overweight infirm man who leaked pus from an old wound. It could not have been pleasant to share a bed with him. The three dashing young courtiers must have been very appealing in contrast.

"Again, many say that there is no way Anne would have taken such a risk. But Anne was daring, adventurous and had been wildly successful. She had enchanted and, by many accounts, driven a King wild with lust. Unlike her sister, and many others, she was not prepared to be just the Kings mistress. It would have seemed a mad idea that Henry would ever divorce Catherine of Aragon to marry her. But he had.

"Anne was the most powerful woman in the land and, at one point at least, Henry had been putty in her hand. But, as we have seen many times, pride comes before a very big fall. People who achieve power often come to think of themselves as untouchable. They then over-reach themselves and are brought crashing to earth. Later in Henry's reign it would happen to Thomas Cromwell who was one of the cleverest men in history. If it could happen to him it could certainly happen to Anne Boleyn.

"Can we really completely discount the idea that Anne just became too reckless and this, along with her desperation for a son, prompted her to take one of the young men who waited upon her every day as a lover?

"I do not think we can. Foreign ambassadors noted the closeness of these men to the Queen. There is a surviving poem by the French ambassador that calls Anne a whore and names Norris and her brother George as her lovers. In the spirit of fairness I would point out that the poem was written three days after Anne's execution. But would the French ambassador have made it up to embarrass Henry? It is quite possible but surely it also served to vindicate the juries guilty verdict. If the French wanted to make mischief, as they often did at this time, surely it would have been better to paint Anne as the victim and Henry the murderous villain?

"And so, to the fifth supposed lover. Mark Smeaton has always been seen as one of history's victims. He was the patsy. This is the narrative. The King wanted out of his second marriage and made sure his chief fixer, Thomas Cromwell, knew this. Cromwell was aware of the flirtatious behaviour between Anne and some gentlemen of the court and of the gossip about them. But the evidence was paper thin and Cromwell knew he couldn't torture members of the nobility to gain a confession.

"And so this is where Smeaton came him. The evidence against him was so weak it doesn't even warrant the use of the word. It was basically that he had looked moody when Anne ignored him and then she had rebuked him for expecting her to treat him, a servant, like she did the nobility.

As a result of this silly little exchange between a servant and his mistress six people were to lose their lives.

"But, weak as the evidence was, it was enough for Cromwell to arrest him, imprison him and then get a confession that also implicated the three courtiers and George Boleyn. He either achieved this by torture, as most believe, or by tricking him into believing he would be spared if he named the others.

"That is the narrative. That is the story that has been passed down the centuries. But is it true? One of the main reasons this sequence of events is not challenged is because of the way Mark Smeaton has always been portrayed in books, movies and even documentaries. He is always the shy, naïve, innocent caught up in affairs he can't understand. He is the idiot used by great men to bring down a Queen. But can that really be true?

"Mark Smeaton was an entertainer. He was a musician. In the modern day he would be a pop star. How many pop stars do you know that are shy and innocent? They are often arrogant and self-obsessed. They are extroverts. And, Ladies and Gentlemen of the jury, women find them very sexy.

"Mark Smeaton was by all accounts very good-looking. He was at the top of his game. He wasn't just a musician, he was a musician at Henry's court. So, there we have it. Smeaton was young, confident, good-looking, successful and talented. Is it so hard to imagine that Anne Boleyn would be attracted to him?

"That doesn't mean she had sex with him of course. But there is evidence that she was often alone with him. We will never know the truth and I suspect the majority would still consider it unlikely. But there is no way anyone can say with any certainty whether she did or didn't. There is too much doubt. Mark Smeaton could have been guilty.

"And that is the Anne Boleyn affair. For centuries, the narrative has been the same. They were trumped up charges and all involved were innocent. Only a few have ever dared challenge this as those that do are often mocked. In a way it is mob rule but the mob is often wrong as they refuse to listen to anyone's opinion.

"In this case they are rarely asked questions that may challenge the narrative as there is little need. All involved are long-dead and it is fairly clear that, even if Henry the 8th wasn't quite as bad as he is portrayed, who really cares?

"But Ladies and Gentlemen of the jury, I am asking you to examine the facts because in this case there is a very big need. A man's soul is at risk here and that man deserves to have a fair trial. And a fair trial in this case means you have to ignore the centuries old narrative and consider the facts. It will be a tough ask but I am sure you will be up to it.

"I will not trouble the court too much with the Anne of Cleves marriage because nothing my client did in this affair would have brought him to this trial. Henry is remembered primarily for his rather ungallant comments about her looks which I think is unfair. After the marriage was annulled Henry, by his generous treatment of her, proved he could act honourably.

"I will also not spend too much time defending my clients conduct in the case of Catherine Howard. Despite the obvious sympathy many have for her we have to acknowledge that most historians consider it very likely that she was guilty as charged. Indeed, all the surviving testimonies point to this unfortunate conclusion.

"She should not have married the King. It may not have been the law at the time, and Henry was certainly mean-spirited to impose it retrospectively, but she must have known she should have revealed her sexual history before the marriage.

"Of course that would have been very hard for a noble lady of good family to do. I also acknowledge the pressure she was under. Her uncle, the Duke of Norfolk, was desperate for the marriage as it would bring him back into the King's favour. But, while we have the upmost sympathy, we must face the fact that she seems a rather foolish girl and one bedazzled by the thought of becoming Queen.

"And even if we blame the Duke of Norfolk and her family for forcing the marriage we can't blame them for her behaviour after the wedding. The Thomas Culpeper affair occurred after the marriage vows. It may well have been a love match and it is quite possible, although I personally doubt it, that sex did not take place. But the fact a love letter from Culpeper, which implicated both of them, was found in her possession is damning.

"It also clears Henry, in law anyway, of any guilt. Witnesses came forward about this affair and past ones but, under the law at the time, the letter would have been enough to condemn her. It spoke of an undying love and the dream of being together. And they could only be together if the King was dead and, as in one aspect of the Anne Boleyn affair, to speak of the Kings death was to wish the Kings death. This was treason.

"I have sympathy for Catherine Howard. As the prosecution said, she was used by men all her life. She is a victim. I also think Henry could have been lenient but I can understand his viewpoint. In his time sparing someone convicted of treason would have been unthinkable.

"No, in the case of Catherine Howard, we have to admit that, although Henry could have acted better, she was guilty as charged and, under the law at the time, that inevitably meant execution.

"This court is unusual in that we are asking you to consider the deeds and motivation of the man alongside the letter of the law. But, in this case at least, the law must be the dominant factor. We may be sympathetic to her plight but we must acknowledge that she broke laws that carried the death penalty. Henry was undoubtedly bitter as he had been humiliated. He had been publicly cuckolded. But, while this bitterness made any chance of mercy unlikely, the person most responsible for Catherine Howards execution was Catherine Howard herself.

"And so, to Henry's 6th and final wife. Again, what is Henry guilty of in this case? What is he even accused of? Catherine Parr should not have married him as she was in love with Thomas Seymour, who she would go onto marry after the King's death. It is often argued that a marriage proposal from the King was akin to a royal command but, in this case, was that really true?

"She was not under the same family pressure Catherine Howard had been. She was a very wealthy widow with strong connections. She was older, wiser and far more intelligent than Catherine Howard. Henry would almost certainly have been angered by her refusal but, after the Howard debacle, would he really have wanted to marry a woman whose heart belonged to someone else?

"From what we know about the subsequent marriage it is clear she knew how to handle Henry. I think it very likely she could have refused him in such a gentle way his pride would not have been hurt. So why didn't she?

"It was because she saw she could gain a lot from the marriage. And not just in lands and jewels. Henry could be incredibly generous to his wives, in the first throes of romance anyway, but I think Catherine was after something much more substantial. I think it possible, and even probable, that she married him to further the Protestant cause.

"Catherine Parr had been born and brought up as a Catholic but, by the time of her marriage to Henry, it was clear she had become very attracted to the new religion. This brought her into conflict with the powerful men who secretly hated the split with the Roman church.

"It is a common misconception that, after Henry declared himself the supreme leader of the Church in his kingdom, England became a Protestant country. It did not. Henry still considered himself a Roman Catholic. There had certainly been changes and the shift to the Protestant church had begun. Men like Thomas Cromwell had ensured that. But Henry had become concerned with the pace of change and this was partly what cost Cromwell his life. He pushed too hard, took one risk too many and over-stepped the mark. And the same very nearly happened to Catherine Parr.

"One night, in a heated discussion with the King, she argued for more changes to the religion. This conversation was over-heard by the Bishop of Winchester, Stephen Gardiner, and when the King was alone, he approached him and declared her words heresy. And Henry agreed and gave permission for an arrest warrant to be made out in Catherine's name.

"We now know that Catherine was tipped off about the warrant. She then managed to gain an audience with the King in which she qualified her remarks and made out they were to distract him from the pain he was feeling from his wound. She said she did not really believe them and conceded that she was just a woman and that Henry's view had to be right as he was much wiser than her. This mollified the King and the warrant was revoked.

"The prosecution paints this episode as showing how volatile Henry could be. A few words from Gardiner had caused the arrest warrant that would have led to execution and a few more words from Catherine had caused it to be lifted.

"But, whatever else he was, Henry Tudor was not stupid. He knew how intelligent Catherine was and he must have known she had believed in her arguments. And that meant that, under the laws of the time, she was guilty of heresy. And that, unless she reneged, probably meant execution.

"So, rather than an example of his volatility, his acceptance of her explanation was an act of mercy. Stephen Gardiner is always seen as the villain of this piece but, while I suspect he was a vile man, he was the man with the law on his side. He was right in that Catherine was guilty of heresy. But Henry chose to protect her.

"Members of the jury, Henry the 8th has been reviled throughout history for his poor treatment of his six wives. Millions of people's first reaction to his name is to claim he murdered all six of them. Even those who have a bit more knowledge condemn him as a man who treated all his wives very badly.

"But let us examine that. For the majority of his first marriage, he treated Catherine of Aragon very well. It is clear that for many years he truly loved her. It was only at the end, when Henry's need to have a son trumped everything else, that it turned toxic. But let us be clear. If she had acceded to his demands, he would have honoured her all her life.

"He treated his third wife, Jane Seymour, very well and it was a tragedy that she died giving birth to his son. His fourth marriage to Anne of Cleves was a ghastly mistake but, although the marriage was annulled very quickly, Henry respected her and upheld her status as a Queen until the day he died. And, as we have just spoken about, he chose to ignore a clear case of heresy from his sixth wife because of the high regard he had for her.

"So the accusation of cruelty to his wives only really applies to two of them. And, while he showed no mercy to Catherine Howard, it is pretty clear she was guilty of adultery and treason. Can he really be called cruel for allowing the law to take its course in such a case? In the 1500's treason was always punished by execution.

"So that only leaves one wife. Henry's bad reputation pretty much comes down to the bloody end of his second marriage to Anne Boleyn. Ministers such as Cromwell and Bishops such as Thomas More were also executed. But holding high office had been a very dangerous occupation for centuries before Henry and would be for centuries after his death.

"You could be riding high one day and have your head on the block the next. But very often these men were technically guilty. Cromwell was certainly guilty of heresy and possibly guilty of corruption. And Thomas More refused to recognise Henry's supremacy in matters of faith.

"We can have sympathy for these men, and many others, as they were undoubtedly treated badly by Henry. But these men knew the dangers of their personal choices. We might not like the laws at the time, or the fact that Henry used it for his own purposes, but we have to accept there were laws and these men broke them. I do not think Henry was any worse in this regard than many monarchs who came before him and after him. I am sure his daughter, Mary, was much worse and Elizabeth had her moments too."

"No, in the way he treated his ministers, advisors and bishop's Henry was no better and no worse than any other monarch of the times.

Lightfoot paused and looked at each member of the jury who, to Henry's eyes, looked spell-bound. Lightfoot walked slowly in a small circle before facing them and continuing.

"It can be argued that Henry's split from the Pope led to thousands of deaths. It is a valid point but breaking free from the rule of a foreign power seems eminently sensible to me. I would argue that, in the centuries since, England has benefited immensely from this decision.

"Henry faced a choice. He could accept the Pope's refusal to annul his first marriage which would mean the end of the Tudor line. Or he could refuse to accept it and claim royal supremacy in matters of religion in his own country. He chose the second and, I for one, do not think that unreasonable. In the centuries since it is obvious that the people supported this decision because, when any monarch has tried to take England back to the Pope, they have been given short shrift.

"So it all comes down to Anne Boleyn and her alleged lovers. This is the affair that brought Henry to this court. But, as I have pointed out, the affair is in no way as clear-cut as history suggests. I again ask you to examine the evidence in a dispassionate way. Ask yourself if you can, in all honesty, conclusively state that Anne and the others were innocent.

"And if you can't you must find Henry not guilty. What happened to Catherine of Aragon, Anne of Cleves, Catherine Howard, Catherine Parr, Thomas Cromwell and Thomas More is of no consequence. It is all about Anne Boleyn."

Lightfoot once more made eye contact with every member of the jury before walking back to his table. He looked at Henry before returning to the centre of the court.

"There is another point I would like to make. It is an event that is well known to historians but only a very few have placed any great significance to it. But, because of the timing of it, it is a very important moment in Henry's life. I would consider it life changing.

"Ladies and Gentlemen of the jury, at the start of this trial the prosecution and myself had a dispute. It was about at which age Henry would appear before you. I wanted a young virile Henry in his early twenties. The prosecution wanted Henry as he was towards the end of his life.

"The reasons for both are obvious. For me, a young handsome Henry would appear a more attractive figure to you the jury. The prosecution wanted the Henry you are most familiar with. The thinking would be that a fat, ugly Henry with his pus-leaking wound would be very unappealing to you and make you more likely to think ill of him. The judge, quite sensibly, compromised at a point in middle age. The date decided upon was Henry's 44th birthday.

"Now, I suspect that Henry's appearance and general demeanour has surprised you in this trial. He is not the raging bully you may have come accustomed to. At times he has lost his temper but we must have some understanding of this. He is under extreme pressure and he is genuinely shocked at how he has been portrayed over the centuries. But where is the famous bombast and arrogance? Where is the famed mental instability? It is not there because the Henry you see before you is not the same man who has been cast as one of the greatest villains in history.

"In the early part of his reign Henry was known for his good-looks, his sporting prowess and his good nature. He was very popular with his subjects and among his courtiers. He was known for his loyalty and good humour. This is light-years from how he has been portrayed. So, what changed?

"History is not wrong in this case. Henry did become quite horrible in his later years. He became obese, angry, frustrated, and vengeful. He lost his ability to emphasise with other people. He became unbalanced, promoting someone to high office one day and then having them executed days later. This happened to Cromwell. The reverse happened to Catherine Parr. She was accused of treason and a day later Henry raged against the men he himself had sent to arrest her. He was undoubtedly mentally unstable at this point.

"But what caused this instability of the mind? I think the first thing modern doctors would look for is massive trauma to the head. And they would find evidence of this very quickly. On the 24th of January 1536 Henry was involved in a jousting tournament. Wearing full armour he was thrown from his horse and then the horse, that was also armoured, fell on top of him. Henry was unconscious for two hours. I believe, Ladies and Gentlemen of the jury, that this accident changed Henry's whole personality. It was the event that turned him into a mentally unbalanced tyrant.

"This is conjecture of course but it is informed conjecture. Modern medical experts on head trauma will tell you that even a five minute period of unconsciousness can cause brain damage and personality change. Henry, by all reports, was unconscious for two hours.

"There are countless examples of personality change after severe head trauma and prolonged unconsciousness. I suspect some of you have had experience of this. Previously kind and thoughtful people can turn into selfish individuals with a total inability to feel sympathy for other people.

"The brain is incredibly complex but we know much more about it now. We know there is a specific part linked to personality and behaviour. We know there is a part that controls emotions. And, Ladies and Gentlemen, of the jury, we know there is a part that allows us to feel empathy for others. And we also know these parts can be changed, damaged or even destroyed entirely by head trauma or prolonged unconsciousness.

"I believe this is maybe what happened to Henry. I also believe the available evidence supports this theory. Henry was a changed man after this accident. There had been plenty of executions before, especially after the break from Rome, but there had been valid reasons for them and, in the high profile ones at least, Henry had tried to avoid them. This changed after the accident.

"I will give you an example. Sir Thomas More had been a close friend but he had refused to recognise the supremacy of the King in matters of religion. As he was Lord Chancellor this was intolerable but Henry gave him every chance to comply with his wishes. He was even told that as long as he didn't speak against the King's supremacy he wouldn't be arrested and would not have to publicly acknowledge it.

"It was only when the high-ranking courtier Richard Rich reported a conversation in which More did speak against the supremacy that Henry authorised his arrest and eventual execution. We may question his willingness to condemn him on the basis of one alleged conversation but compare his actions in this case, which was prior to his accident, with his behaviour after it.

"Henry Norris, Sir Francis Weston and William Brereton had been close friends with Henry for many years. They were trusted, loyal and discreet. But when they were accused, on miniscule evidence, of being the Queen's lovers they were executed within days with Henry not once even questioning their guilt.

"And later Thomas Cromwell, who was as close to the King as anyone could be, was executed almost on a whim after making one mistake. Within days Henry was lamenting his loss.

"He had the teenage Catherine Howard executed with no thought for the horrendous way she had been abused and used all her life. Catherine Parr, who Henry was on very good terms with, was ordered to be arrested because one jealous courtier spoke against her. She survived because the next morning she found Henry in a better mood.

"Ladies and Gentlemen of the jury, these are not the actions of a rational man. And rational is the key word here. During the long war of the roses, and long after it, there were loads of executions and most of these were of men falsely accused of treason. To put it bluntly most of them were pure and simple murders.

"But there was a reason for them. The Kings who ordered them were killers, but they were rational killers. Two young princes were murdered in the tower of London. The most likely perpetrator of this crime is Richard the Third but it may well have been carried out on the orders of Henry the 7th, our Henry's father. It is a disgusting crime but neither Richard or Henry could have been King if it hadn't been carried out. There was a logic to it. It was rational.

"Kings in the 15th and 16th century were brutal and without mercy but they were rational. They would not have survived if they hadn't been. And Henry the 8th was no exception. The execution of Thomas More proves that but this changed after his accident. Before his decisions were shrewd and thought out but afterwards, he was haphazard, inconsistent, and reckless. He had stopped being rational.

"This is most obvious in the Anne Boleyn case. If you still believe they were trumped up charges just to get rid of Anne why were five alleged lovers needed? You could argue that the musician Smeaton might not have been enough but why not him and one of the esteemed courtiers? That would have been more believable. The public, and history itself, might have accepted that. But history was always unlikely to accept that a 16th century Queen would be stupid enough to have sexual relations with five different men. It is irrational.

"But, by this time, Henry was not rational. He was a changed man and what changed him may well have been the jousting accident. He was completely lacking in empathy for other people afterwards. He was selfish in the extreme. He was self-centred and brutal. He was the monster we have come to know from the history books. But he had not always been like that. Once he had been a decent man.

"So, if you still believe he is as guilty as history has decided, does this accident, and the personality-changing effects it had on him, mean he should be forgiven?

"No, of course it does not. He still signed those death warrants. He did not question Cromwell when he arrested three of his best friends on very little evidence. He still condemned to death the foolish young girl, Catherine Howard. I have argued in this trial that all may well have been guilty but, if I have not convinced you, Henry's accident cannot absolve him of the crimes you deem him guilty of.

"But consider this. If a President, a Prime Minister or even a modern-day King had conducted themselves in such an irrational way after major head-trauma they would have been removed from office. It would be decided that they were no longer mentally fit to govern. They would be removed so they were not a danger to their country, their people and themselves.

"And this is what should have happened here. After the accident that left him unconscious for two hours Henry the 8th was no longer fit to govern his country. He should have been saved from himself.

"But of course this was not possible. In 1536 England there was no mechanism to get rid of a King other than a civil war. Presidents can be impeached and Prime Ministers simply voted out by their own parties. Modern day monarchs can be told to step aside by their own parliaments and if they refuse it means the end of monarchy in that nation. But Henry was the ultimate power in the land and he was King until death. No one could tell him to step aside and expect to live very long.

"And so Henry ploughed on with his reign, ordering the arrest of someone one day and pardoning them the next and executing his most loyal friends on a whim. And no, he should not be forgiven for his behaviour but surely his accident and descent into a type of madness must warrant some mitigation.

"It would be wrong to say he was not responsible for his actions but he had been brain damaged. How can we condemn him for showing Catherine Howard no sympathy when the part of his brain that allowed him to feel such an emotion had been completely destroyed?"

Lightfoot paused and looked at each juror in turn before continuing.

"So, there we have it. As jurors you have much to consider. I believe it is far from clear that Henry is guilty of any crime at all. He was certainly harsh and he clearly should have asked more questions. He almost certainly turned a deaf ear to the voice in his head that must have been raising doubts about the guilt of some of the accused. He saw and heard what he wanted to hear. If an accusation of treason was made, which would inevitably lead to execution, he was not going to challenge it if it allowed him to achieve his goals.

"But does this make him guilty of multiple murders? Henry played no part in the trials and never publicly accused anyone. Now, it is a compelling argument that this matters little as everyone seemed to be doing exactly what he wanted. The narrative is that Henry made clear what he wanted and people like Thomas Cromwell made it happen.

"It is a powerful argument, and it is how these events are remembered by history. But none of us can be sure that it is true. By modern standards a Tudor court of law appears very unfair to the accused. And, in a case of treason brought by the King's first minister, a jury would be under the most extreme pressure imaginable to bring in the verdict that minister wanted.

"But by 1536 England had had a functioning legal system for several hundred years. There were hundreds of lawyers, some of whom had studied law at the best universities in the World.

"And consider this. Thomas Cromwell was denied a trial when he himself was accused of treason and with good reason. He was recognised as the foremost lawyer in the land. The man was undoubtedly brilliant and his accusers feared he would run rings round the prosecution lawyer and be acquitted. To avoid any chance of this they got parliament to find him guilty without a trial. Doesn't this show that Tudor courts were prepared to listen to defence-arguments and act independently?"

"And, Ladies and Gentlemen of the jury, if you are still not convinced by my arguments you still have to decide how much guilt he truly carries. Yours is a challenging task. Henry the 8th did not actually kill anyone. He was never the hangman or the headsman. Most of the men and women who were executed had a trial. We may certainly question the fairness of those trials but they were conducted under the legal system of the time. Those that did not receive a trial were executed after parliament passed laws.

"Of course history has decided that all this does not matter as the courts and parliament just did what Henry wanted them to. It is a fair and, given the evidence, entirely understandable viewpoint. But we cannot be sure. We cannot be sure of many things.

"I don't think we can be sure that Henry wasn't entirely convinced of their guilt. And this matters because if Henry was truly convinced of their guilt surely we cannot label him a murderer. Even if this was a false belief we have to accept he believed them guilty of treason and the only punishment for treason was death.

"Now, you may question if he did genuinely believe it. What rational man could so easily believe his wife was having sexual relations with three of his best friends, a servant and her own brother? Would a sane man not question the convenience of these charges in that they freed him to marry again?

"Of course they would but, as I have pointed out, after his accident Henry was not rational or sane. He was brain damaged. So, members of the jury, would it be so surprising that a brain damaged man could be so lacking in judgement? Is it so unbelievable that a man with such a flawed brain could be convinced of even the most unlikely of charges?"

Lightfoot paused and walked back to his table. He leant back against it and then continued.

"Members of the jury, if you still believe that most of the high-profile people who were executed during the reign of Henry the 8th were innocent the question you ultimately have to ask yourself is this. How much guilt should a brain damaged King carry if he did truly believe they were guilty of adultery and treason?

"I put it to you that history has been somewhat unkind to Henry the 8th. There are three things to consider. First, can you be sure, beyond any reasonable doubt, that all those executed were innocent of the crimes they were accused of? I do not believe anyone can be. If you share that belief you must find the defendant not guilty.

"If you are sure that all were innocent victims of plotters and that they all faced trumped up charges you must consider this. Was Henry himself the chief architect of those plots? Just because he benefited from the deaths doesn't mean he planned them. I don't think we can convict Henry of Anne Boleyn's death just because he had told Thomas Cromwell he regretted the marriage. I find that ludicrous and if you agree with me you must find the defendant not guilty.

"If you still believe Henry is responsible for the deaths of so many innocents I would ask you to take into consideration his impaired mental state after his serious head injury. I would suggest the accident left him with an inability to sympathise with others. I think it also caused him to be easily manipulated by clever men like Cromwell and the Duke of Norfolk.

"This last consideration is more difficult. You may believe he was mentally damaged but still feel he carries direct responsibility for multiple executions of innocent people. But is that fair? In modern courts a defendant's mental state is taken into account. Many found guilty of murders are sent to psychiatric hospitals rather than prison. Even in countries with the death penalty defendants with mental illness are not executed. There is an acceptance that their crimes would probably not have been committed if they had their mental faculties intact.

"Ladies and Gentlemen of the jury, are we to deny Henry the same consideration? He is already dead. He has been so for 450 years. But you must decide if he should suffer a fate worse than death. Your task is to decide if Henry is indeed the monster portrayed in the history books. He has been found guilty by history and you are being asked to rubber-stamp that verdict and send his soul to hell.

"I personally do not believe there is enough evidence to convict him in any case. But if I have not convinced you I urge you to consider the considerable evidence that suggests he was mentally disturbed when the alleged crimes took place. And, if you believe that mental disturbance played a large part in those alleged crimes, you must surely find the defendant not guilty."

Lightfoot turned to the judge.

"That concludes my final arguments My Lord."

Amira Hussein stood up.

"I know this is unusual at this point My lord, but I have an objection."

The judge nodded.

"I am pretty sure I know what that objection will be but go ahead."

"The council for the defence has introduced an element into his closing arguments that played no part in the trial. At no point did he mention the jousting accident and this allowed me no chance to question the claim that this had an effect on the defendant's personality and behaviour."

"I agree. Mr Lightfoot you were out of order, and I will now take the unusual step of allowing the prosecution to challenge your theory. Do you need time Miss Hussein to prepare that challenge?

"No, My Lord."

"Then please proceed."

Amira Hussein turned towards the jury.

"Ladies and Gentlemen of the jury, let us be clear on one thing. When the defence council states that medical experts would testify that even a five minute period of unconsciousness can cause brain damage and personality change he is not wrong. And he is also correct in stating that Henry was unconscious for at least two hours.

"But does this prove that Henry suffered brain damage or personality change? No, it does not because there is a key word in his statement. It is a small, and he would like you to believe, insignificant word. He placed no emphasis on it. He brushed over the word hoping you wouldn't notice it. That word is "can".

"Every medical expert in the world will tell you that any head trauma can cause brain damage and personality change. They will also state that the longer a person is unconscious the bigger the danger of this happening. But Ladies and Gentlemen of the jury, they will also state the exact opposite. They will say that a person can experience both severe head trauma and prolonged unconsciousness without any long-lasting effects.

"Two hours of unconsciousness is indeed a long time but there are numerous examples of people regaining consciousness after much longer periods and making a full recovery. Some people have been in a coma for years before recovering without any side-effects.

"I do not have the data to indicate if a person is likely or less likely to experience brain damage or personality change after two hours of unconsciousness. But when you consider how many boxers, footballers, rugby players, racing drivers and workmen have survived massive head trauma I suspect it is the latter. Even if I am wrong it would at best be 50/50.

"The defence council is clearly wrong to present this as a given fact. Henry may have suffered brain damage and personality change as a result of his accident. But equally, he may not have. It is a theory at best and I don't think the facts support this theory.

"And I am not alone in this belief. It is not a new theory. You may wonder why I turned down the chance to take some time to prepare my rebuttal of this claim. It is because I had already prepared it as I suspected the defence would at some point make this claim. The fact that they tried to sneak it in during closing arguments rather than during cross-examination suggests to me that they know how weak that claim is.

"The reason why you have probably not heard of this theory is because it has never reached the mainstream. And the reason for this is because most historians have rejected it. And, when you examine the evidence, you can see why.

"Henry was a different man after the accident but it was not damage to the brain that caused this change. It was the physical injuries to his body that caused him distress for the rest of his life. He could no longer take part in the tournaments and he found riding so painful that he eventually stopped even that. He grew fat and his leg seeped pus. He also suffered from gout among various other ailments.

"This man, who had prided himself on his physical fitness and athleticism, became an embittered, frustrated, fat old man before his time. And embittered frustrated men often lash out and blame others for their misfortune. They want to see others suffer as they suffer. Henry the 8th didn't become irrational. He became bad.

"The defence has focused on the Anne Boleyn execution along with her alleged lovers. I do not disagree with this but I do disagree that Henry's actions were irrational and were a direct result of his accident just a couple of weeks before.

"Henry wanted out of his marriage and he charged Thomas Cromwell with getting him out as quickly as possible. This was a very rational decision as Cromwell was brilliant and had made Henry's split from his first marriage to Catherine of Aragon possible. But Henry was faced with another decision when Cromwell told him that Anne had committed adulterous treason with four nobles, three of whom were close friends, and one servant.

"I will never believe that Henry really thought they were all guilty but what was he to do? If he refused to believe it that would mean he was accusing Cromwell of lying and this would be treason. And Cromwell, his most brilliant advisor, would be executed. And at the end of all that Henry would still be married to Anne Boleyn. But if he chooses to believe Cromwell, Anne Boleyn is executed, and Henry is free to marry Jane Seymour. He also gets to keep his first minister.

"The defence says that allowing five lovers to be falsely accused was irrational as very few would be likely to believe it. But the defence is wrong. Henry's choice was to believe Cromwell and get all he wanted or not to believe him and stay married to Anne while losing his chief minister. And so, Henry took the rational decision. He believed Cromwell and in doing so authorised multiple state murders.

"Henry the 8th was not brain-damaged or irrational. He was just easily manipulated by clever men like Cromwell and powerful men like Norfolk. And he was manipulated before the accident as well as after it. The only genuinely irrational act I can see is the execution of Cromwell himself. But this was caused by his anger at Cromwell's mistake in making the Anne of Cleves marriage along with Norfolk's scheming. And even rational men make irrational decisions when angry and embittered.

"Marrying Catherine Howard may have seemed irrational but, let's face it, millions of rich middle-aged men hook up with women young enough to be their daughters. It is called a mid-life crisis. It is not irrational. It is not because of brain-damage. It is just sad and a little pathetic. Sadly, it is also fairly normal behaviour. What is not normal is chopping their heads off when you discover that they really do prefer men of their own age. No, just very evil men do that.

"And after Catherine Howard he did what human beings tend to do and lurched from one extreme to the other. Where Catherine Howard had been young and foolish Catherine Parr was older, experienced, even-tempered, and wise. This is not irrational behaviour brought on by head trauma. It is normal human behaviour."

She paused and looked at Henry, the judge and Lightfoot before turning back to the jury.

"No, Ladies and Gentlemen of the jury, Henry and his defence team cannot use his jousting accident as an excuse for his murderous behaviour. When he allowed his second wife and three of his friends to be executed he was completely sane and in control of his actions. He must have had had serious doubts as to their guilt but he didn't care as their deaths benefited him. Henry never cared about anyone but himself. All lives were forfeit if it suited him. No one was safe. Not his wife, ministers friends or family."

She again paused but for the first time she did what Lightfoot had continually done and made eye contact with all the jurors. And then she continued.

"Ladies and Gentlemen of the jury, Henry the 8th was a monster and he was a sane monster. There is no mitigation or excuses for his crimes. He was a murderous evil tyrant and you must find him guilty of all charges."

She turned to the judge.

"That concludes my rebuttal My Lord."

"Thank you, Miss Hussein. The court will adjourn before my summing up."

Chapter Twenty-Five

Judges summing up

Henry, like everyone else in the room, stood as the judge entered through a side-door. He had done so from the start of the trial. The first time he had been directed to do so he had obeyed the instruction through his confusion at the strangeness of it all. But that didn't explain why he had continued to do so without complaint. When had he got so meek and compliant? He, the King of England, should not stand for anyone.

The judge took his seat and everyone, including Henry, did the same. The judge straightened some notes on his desk and then looked at the jury.

"Ladies and Gentlemen of the jury, first I would like to thank you for your dedicated attention throughout the trial. It is a difficult case which you have treated with due seriousness and your concentration has not wavered. But I would ask you to keep that concentration up as I am about to give you another very difficult task.

"This case can be simple or complex. If you came to this trial convinced that Henry the 8th is the murderous tyrant portrayed in the history books, and nothing that has been said here has changed that opinion, your task is easy. You will find the defendant guilty. If the defence has raised doubts the case becomes much more complicated.

"If this is the case you have much to consider. First and foremost you must decide on the fairness of the various trials. Technically, and in law, Henry is not guilty of any crime. Everything was done in line with the legal system of the time. But you may decide that this legal system was so weighted in favour of the rich and powerful that it was little more than a sham.

"There is ample circumstantial evidence of this. The verdict on Henry will be decided by the twelve of you and you all come from diverse backgrounds and represent the whole of society. This was far from the case in the trials of Anne Boleyn and her alleged lovers. Their fate was decided by a few high ranking members of the nobility. You may consider that these men, who owed their position to the King, might be under extreme pressure to bring in the verdict that the King desired.

"But, if you do decide this you then have to ask yourselves two questions. The first would be whether the accused were in fact guilty or not guilty. Just because you consider the legal system unfair to the accused does not mean that legal system got it wrong. Just because you think the jury, if you could call it such, brought in the verdict the King wanted it does not mean that verdict was wrong.

"This consideration is going to be difficult as you cannot fail to be influenced by history's portrayal of these events: a portrayal that normally suggests that most of those condemned to die were innocent. But, while I acknowledge the difficulty, I urge you to try to keep an open mind and study the evidence and arguments presented by both the prosecution and the defence.

"The second question you have to ask yourself is this. If you consider the trials a sham, and the executions basically state murder, how culpable is Henry the 8th? He did not wield the axe. He did not pronounce them guilty. He did not even accuse or charge them. How much guilt should he carry?

"As both the prosecution and defence have mainly focused on the Anne Boleyn affair I will do the same but my comments are relevant to all of Henry's alleged crimes. These are the facts as I see them.

"Henry the 8th wanted out of his marriage to Anne Boleyn. He made this clear to his chief minister, Thomas Cromwell. Soon after this Cromwell supposedly heard rumours of inappropriate behaviour between Anne and several male courtiers. He conducted an investigation which resulted in the arrest, trial and execution of Anne and five men. And, at the end of this, Henry had the wish, that he had expressed to Cromwell just weeks before, come true.

"If you are not persuaded by the defence's argument that they might well have been guilty as charged you must decide if Henry or Cromwell was responsible for the false charges, the false convictions and the false executions. You may decide both were. Henry got what he wanted and did not question how Cromwell had managed it. But does that make him culpable? You must decide.

"The fate of Catherine Howard is more clear-cut but, because of the nature of this court, it should not be down-played. In a normal trial I would say there was no case to answer. Most historians consider Catherine Howard guilty as charged and the available evidence supports this. But this is not a normal trial.

"You are basically being asked to decide if Henry the 8th is the murderous tyrant portrayed in the history books. In the Anne Boleyn case you have to judge if he caused the death of six people while knowing they were innocent. That is relatively straightforward but other things Henry is accused of are more complex and Catherine Howard's execution is one of them.

"It basically comes down to this. Even though legally he was within his rights to have her executed, did he really have to do so. Could he not show a little mercy to a teenage girl who had been abused and used all her life. Was it morally right? What would it have cost him to show her mercy?

"We also have to consider Henry's very active role in the execution of Lady Jane Rochford. She was Catherine Howard's lady in waiting and, allegedly, aided and protected Catherine in her adulterous relationship with Thomas Culpeper. After suffering a nervous break-down following weeks of fierce interrogation she was declared insane. This meant she could not be tried in a court of law. But Henry got parliament to pass a law that said that an insane person could be tried and executed for high-treason.

"Now, as a legal man, I find this the most serious charge against Henry. In all the other cases it is not clear that Henry caused their deaths. In the Anne Boleyn case it might well be Thomas Cromwell that carried most responsibility. But the case of Jane Rochford is different. She died because Henry wanted her to die and he abused his power to make this happen. Now, you may decide his actions were understandable as Jane was almost certainly guilty as charged. But you may also consider this is another reason why Henry the 8th is considered an evil monster.

"In regard to his marriage to Catherine of Aragon I would ask you to separate the personal from the political. His need for a divorce was personal and his split from the church of Rome was political. The personal crisis led to the political one but, to be sure of a fair trial, we must examine them separately. You must also scrutinise Henry's behaviour over a prolonged period.

"From a personal stand-point Henry had to divorce Catherine. She was past child-bearing age and she had not given birth to a son. If Henry did not marry again the Tudor line would end.

"Now we may condemn Henry for this, and he was of course in a relationship with Anne Boleyn, but we must recognise his motivation and real need for the divorce. It is morally very questionable but it hardly makes him a monster.

You may also think it likely, as I do, that he would have treated Catherine well if she had gone along with his plans.

"Now this could be considered a poor decision on her part but the evidence suggests that this deeply religious woman just refused to lie. Henry needed her to state on oath that her first marriage to Henry's elder brother Arthur had been consummated. This she refused to do and, as this was a woman who truly feared God's wrath, we have to suspect it was not consummated.

"So, Henry behaved very badly and his treatment of Catherine after the divorce was cruel in the extreme. She was kept as a prisoner for the rest of her life and was even refused visits from her daughter. But, as the defence has pointed out, it might well have been dangerous to allow her freedom. There was huge opposition to Henry's new Church of England and Catherine would possibly have become a focal point for rebellion. Does this excuse his cruelty? This is what you must decide.

"Now we must examine the political ramifications of Henry's decision to break with the church of Rome. It is beyond doubt that he did it in order to divorce Catherine of Aragon and marry Anne Boleyn. But there were other elements at play here. Henry was not used to not getting his own way and the Pope's refusal to grant an annulment must have brought home to him that he, despite being King of England, was not the ultimate power in the land.

"In modern times we have an image of the Pope as a kindly old man dispensing wisdom to his billions of followers. He is the ultimate authority on the religious doctrine of the Roman Catholic church, but he does not interfere with the internal politics of the many nations whose people are overwhelmingly followers of his faith. It was different in the 1500's. To be a Pope then you also had to be a politician and military leader.

"As the defence has pointed out, at the time Henry asked the Pope to annul his first marriage the pontiff was a virtual prisoner of the holy Roman emperor. The Kingdoms of Spain and France, both of whom had a strained relationship with the English crown, also had enormous influence on the Pope. Considering all this you might well conclude that England was, to a certain extent, in the power of long-term European rivals and, despite his personal reasons, Henry was right to remove England from that foreign influence.

"Now, it is for you to decide if these political considerations excuse his personal selfishness in the split from the Roman Catholic church. And, make no mistake, his actions caused absolute terror among his subjects. In Henry's time religion was all powerful and nearly everyone believed they had a mortal soul and any change in their religious practices could result in eternal damnation.

"We know many chose to be burnt at the stake rather than recognise Henry as leader of the church in England over the Pope. We also know that thousands were killed on both sides as England lurched from one side to the other following Henry's death. Again, you must decide on how much responsibility Henry carries for these deaths and if removing England from foreign influence justified his actions.

"But when you consider this you must not let yourself be influenced by two popular misconceptions that have developed over the centuries.

"First off, Henry did not turn England into a Protestant country when he split from the Church of Rome. In certain times he has been called the first Protestant King but that is false. His son, Edward, has this distinction. It is without doubt that Henry's decision hurried England down the path to becoming a Protestant Country but that was never his intention. Right up to his death people were executed for heresy for preaching Protestant views. Thomas Cromwell was, in part, convicted so. The split from Rome was about Royal supremacy in religious matters in England. But Henry the 8th was born a Catholic and he died a Catholic.

"Another misconception is that the centuries old conflict between the Roman Catholic and Protestant religions started with Henry's decision to break from the Church of Rome. It did not. Religious persecutions, mass slaughters and wars had been raging in Europe since 1517 when a German professor of moral theology called Martin Luther published a document that was heavily critical of the Catholic church and its practices. A powerful country like England eventually adopting the Protestant faith was a massive boost to it, and this may never have happened without Henry's decision, but he did not start the conflict."

The judge put his papers together and then gave a grim smile to the jury.

"So, there we have it. The prosecution have made their case and the defence has countered it. I have outlined both arguments as well as I can and I have given you guidelines and asked you to consider certain things. It is now up to you. Take your time and go through all the arguments carefully.

"The question you must answer is clear. It is simply this. Does Henry the 8th deserve to be remembered as a monster for the whole of eternity or has he been unfairly treated by history. I leave it for you to decide.

Chapter Twenty-Six

The Verdict

Henry watched the jury file in. He studied their faces and general demeanour, but he gleaned nothing from doing so. He wondered if it was just these people, who were born nearly half a millennium after him, that he found so difficult to read or had he always been out of touch with ordinary people.

He felt nervous. No, that was not true. He felt scared. The verdict should not have bothered him so. What did it matter if these people found him guilty? He had been dead for 450 years and he would continue to be dead whatever the verdict. The whole thing was a meaningless sham. That is what he had told Lightfoot. So why did he care? Why was he scared?

Lightfoot had smiled at his bombast.

"You care all right Henry. Admit it, you hate how you have been portrayed all these centuries. You considered yourself to have been a fair monarch and a good man but history has decided that you are the very opposite of fair and just. You are considered an evil monster and that horrifies you. You may say you don't care what people think of you but you do. Many, both alive and dead, say that but for 95% of people it is a lie.

"Now you have had a chance to put your side. You have been able to defend yourself and you know that a not guilty verdict might mean future generations may think better of you. But what terrifies you, or at least makes you very nervous, is that these 12 people will not accept your defence and the view history has of you will stay the same. Your fear is nothing to be ashamed of. If I was you I would be just as scared. Anyone would be."

And Lightfoot had been right. Henry did care. He cared very much. What man would truly be happy to be condemned as a murderous monster?

He watched the jury take their seats and then Lightfoot and Amira Hussein, with their assistants, came in. They glanced and then nodded to each other but Henry gleaned nothing from this as both looked calm and blank-faced.

He had asked Lightfoot if he was confident of the outcome but his response had been far from re-assuring.

"I am neither confident nor nervous. We have done all we can and you presented yourself well. Now we can only wait and hope for the best."

"I think they will find me guilty."

"Why do you think that?"

"Because it is not fair. What can these people truly know of being a King in the 16ᵗʰ century. They do not know what it takes to win and keep a crown against powerful enemies and traitors."

"True, but do you not think it was fairer than the trials in your day?"

"You are right but it still does not make it truly fair."

"I agree but it is as fair as we can get it."

"It is just a game between you and that woman. If the jury believes you, I am not guilty and I am guilty if they believe her."

"Is that really why you think they might find you guilty?"
Henry hesitated.

"Yes of course. It is not fair."
Lightfoot smiled.

"I do not think so Henry. That is not why you fear a guilty verdict."

"Then why do I?"

Lightfoot smiled again.

"You fear it Henry because, having looked at the evidence, you are no longer sure of your own innocence."

Henry stared at him for several seconds.

"It is hard being a King. But if you are right what chance do I have? If even I have doubt in my mind how can they not find me guilty?"

Lightfoot smiled again.

"You may well be right Henry but, unlike your courts, it is up to the prosecution to prove your guilt beyond reasonable doubt. So, if there is doubt, you should have the benefit of it."

"But does that always happen?"

This time Lightfoot's smile was grimmer.

"No Henry, I am afraid it does not. And of course, we may not have done enough to raise doubt."

And now, as Henry stood as the judge took his seat, he felt desolate. He still considered it unfair to be judged by these people but the fact they were doing so made one thing very clear. Whether he was guilty of letting innocent people be killed or not, one fact could not be denied. His reign had been a failure.

All his father had fought for had been lost in two generations. In truth it had been lost in one. His daughter Elizabeth had by all accounts been a mighty monarch but her sex meant that the Tudor line had to end with her death. No, he Henry, had failed to build on his Father's legacy.

And even if God had decided to deny him a male heir, he could have accepted this judgment better. He could have served his country and the Tudor name better. But, in his anger and frustration, he had lashed out at the people who could have helped make this happen. He had made foolish decisions.

Cromwell had come into his life and made him, and England, rich. But Henry had allowed him to be killed and in the years after his death both Henry and his country became much poorer. Cromwell was guilty as charged but that did not make it any less foolish. He had been weak and easily manipulated all his reign. He had been a failure.

The judge took his seat, and everyone followed suit. Henry looked at the jury, but none would meet his eye. Surely that could not be a good sign.

But did Henry's failure and weakness make him a murderous monster? Was history, right? Did he turn a blind eye to loyal friends being executed because it suited him? He told himself that no, he just did what had to be done. Everyone was guilty as charged and if people lived in terror of him it was because of their own treasonous thoughts. But there was doubt in his own mind now.

The judge turned to the jury.

"Ladies and Gentlemen of the jury, have you elected a foreman?"

A man at the front stood up.

"We have your honour."

"And have you reached a verdict on which all twelve of you are agreed?

"We have your honour."

Henry had never been more frightened. His heart was beating out of his chest. Surely, they would be merciful.

"And do you find the defendant, Henry Tudor, guilty or not guilty?

The man hesitated and Henry dared not even breathe. And then the man spoke.

"We the jury find Henry Tudor….

You decide. You are the Jury.

Your verdicts can be sent to my facebook page.

https://www.facebook.com/profile.php?id=10006 4335060865

Also by this Author

The Cursed Sister
http://www.amazon.com/dp/b0844jwmpm

The Viennese Candidate
http://www.amazon.com/dp/b08stzgv5c

The Boy on the Beach
http://www.amazon.com/dp/b07hnfjrk8

Printed in Great Britain
by Amazon